Blaze

Dear Reader,

This book holds a special place in my heart because, well...Taylor is me. I didn't come from a rich family or anything as she does, but my first love hailed from career military stock and his family thought a bohemian artistic type wasn't the right match for their son, who was on a fast-track medical career in the air force. He, being a dutiful son, broke my heart and went on to achieve much success in the air force.

I hate to say how long ago that first love was, but you know, you never forget your first. I moved on and eventually found my true Prince Charming and never looked back. But when I was trying to come up with an idea for a driven, career air force doctor, that first love popped into my head. And as writers tend to do, I started wondering, *what if.*

The Right Stuff is my fantasy of how that romance might have played out if life had taken a different twist. So in that respect, I'm Taylor and Daniel is my first love. So cast your mind back to your own true love and come play *what if* with me as Taylor and Daniel mend the old wounds and learn that they do indeed have the right stuff to make their romance work.

Best wishes,

Lori Wilde

The Right Stuff

LORI WILDE

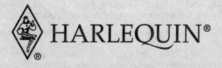

HARLEQUIN®

TORONTO • NEW YORK • LONDON
AMSTERDAM • PARIS • SYDNEY • HAMBURG
STOCKHOLM • ATHENS • TOKYO • MILAN • MADRID
PRAGUE • WARSAW • BUDAPEST • AUCKLAND

Recycling programs
for this product may
not exist in your area.

ISBN-13: 978-0-373-79467-6
ISBN-10:   0-373-79467-3

THE RIGHT STUFF

www.eHarlequin.com

Printed in U.S.A.

ABOUT THE AUTHOR

Lori Wilde is the author of forty books. She's been nominated for a RITA® Award and four *Romantic Times BOOKreviews* Reviewers' Choice Awards. Her books have been excerpted in *Cosmopolitan, Redbook* and *Quick & Simple.* Lori teaches writing online through Ed2go. She's an R.N. trained in forensics, and she volunteers at a battered women's shelter.

Books by Lori Wilde

To FPG. You know who you are.

1

Thirteen years earlier

NEWLY MINTED air force Second Lieutenant Daniel Corben fisted his hand around the black velvet ring box in the pocket of the dress blues he'd worn to his graduation ceremony at the University of Texas. All he could think about was ditching his adoring family so he could be alone with Taylor.

Taylor Milton, twenty, red-haired, a regal beauty. She stood near the end of the reception hall of the ROTC building in a white dress so thin he could see the shape of her thighs through the gauzy material. She gave him a come-hither smile, then coyly dipped her head, but she never took her eyes off him.

His throat constricted and his groin squeezed.

What a woman.

Just looking at her—tall, curvy, sassy and smart—caused his heart to chug as though he was running track. He couldn't help noticing that every masculine gaze in the place landed on her. Taylor was the kind of woman who commanded attention.

And she belonged to him.

Smugness swelled his chest. He tightened his grip

on the box containing the three-quarter-carat diamond solitaire set in platinum and gold that he'd bought that morning. In two weeks he would report to the Uniformed Services University of the Health Sciences at the Bethesda Medical Center near Washington, D.C., to start his medical school training.

But he wanted his ring on Taylor's finger before he left. He wished he could afford something bigger. As it was, he'd drained his savings account to pay for it. He knew she could buy her own ring worth ten times as much as this one and he felt a little insecure about that. Still, he was giving her his all. The very best he could do. He was certain she'd appreciate that. He would promise her that after he was through medical school, he'd buy her a proper diamond.

Daniel's mother reached up to brush a hand over his shoulder, her eyes misting with tears. "I'm so proud of you," she murmured.

"Aw, Mom, don't cry."

His mother swiped at her face and smiled widely. "They're happy tears."

"Keeping up family tradition." His father thumped him on the back with a hammy palm. "You're a true Corben, son. Following in the footsteps of history."

"All my friends think you're hot." His sixteen-year-old sister Jenna giggled. "An airman and a doctor. Oo-la-la."

"I'm not a doctor yet," Daniel reminded her. His family tended to get carried away with military medicine. "I've got four years of medical school, an internship and a residency ahead of me."

"But you're on your way," said his grandfather, retired air force Colonel Dr. Daniel Walter Corben,

Senior, who was also best friends with a former Surgeon General. "Just stay true to your objectives, hold the course. You'll make it."

"We've got dinner reservations at the Rivera," his mother said. "We'd better get a move on. Are you riding with us or taking your car?"

"Um, Mom…" Daniel began, realizing that what he was about to say was going to go over like a cast-iron balloon. "I'm afraid I've got other plans."

A frown creased his mother's forehead as she tracked his gaze to Taylor. She pressed her lips into a tight line. "Of course you do. How presumptuous of me to assume you'd spend the evening of your college graduation with your family."

"Pamela." His father took his mother's elbow. "Daniel is an adult. He has other plans. Let it go."

No one suggested that Taylor join them. Daniel didn't miss the slight. He knew what his family thought about his girlfriend, but for the first time in his life he didn't let their opinion sway him. "We'll go out tomorrow," he promised. "My treat."

His mother turned away, shoulders slumping, her feelings hurt. He took a deep breath.

They disliked Taylor because she was flamboyant, impulsive, opinionated and passionate about the things she believed in. They warned him that a woman like Taylor would be a liability for a career military officer who had to toe the line and be part of a team. He needed a wife who could do the same. Taylor spoke her mind when a proper military wife would find a discreet way to get her point across. She didn't kowtow to everyone and the military was all about kowtowing.

During the short time he'd known her, Taylor had been arrested when a campus protest against the policies of the White House had gotten out of hand, ended up on probation for a streaking stunt gone awry and she'd written an inflammatory letter to the local newspaper espousing her liberal views—his parents were staunch conservatives—and she wasn't about to back down.

But her passionate nature was one of the things he loved most about her. She had a mind of her own and she wasn't afraid to use it and she really didn't care what other people thought of her. He'd never expected to fall in love with someone his parents disapproved of, but it had happened and he wasn't going to apologize.

His father shot him a look that said, *Give your mother some time. She'll come around,* and then he escorted her from the reception hall.

After his family departed, Daniel turned to find Taylor standing in front of him, a naughty twinkle in her eye. "Hey," he said.

"Hey." She grinned.

For a moment they just stood there looking, lost in each other's eyes.

"Come on," she said, reaching out to take his hand. "I have a surprise."

He sank his hand in hers and let her lead him through the crowd of military graduates and out the back exit. The woman was a force of nature, impossible to resist.

She took him up the back stairs of the ROTC building.

"Where are we going?" he asked.

"No questions," she said in a mysterious voice that sent anticipation jolting up his spine.

Daniel watched her butt sway as they climbed, past

the second, the third, the fourth floors, the fifth, apparently headed for the roof. Her high heels tapped seductively against the cement. The sight of her firm fanny moving beneath the thin cotton material of her dress heated his dick as surely as the caress of her hand.

No way was he going off to D.C. leaving Taylor in Texas to finish up her odd double major in theatre and human biology without at least getting engaged. They belonged together and he wanted everyone to know it.

The stairwell was warm, airless, and so was Daniel's brain.

Four months they'd known each other, having met at a campus mixer. Not long enough, most people might say. But in his heart, he knew she was the one. And it wasn't just the sex, although the sex was spectacular. He'd never known anyone as uninhibited in bed—or out of it for that matter—as his Taylor. They'd made love in every position conceivable. She gave as good as she got. Hell, she gave better than she got.

He wanted her so badly his entire body ached. He wanted her naked.

Now.

Of course if it was up to him, he'd keep her naked 24-7. Taylor however, liked to role-play. She enjoyed props and costumes. He'd seen her in a French maid's outfit and a nurse's uniform and a belly dancer's get-up with tiny cymbals on her fingers. But what appealed to him most was her soft bare skin, porcelain white in its naked perfection.

She pushed through the door leading to the roof and stopped just long enough to toss him a seductive look over her shoulder. Her long red hair moved, tumbling around her shoulders like a fiery waterfall. She gave him a sly wink. "Close your eyes."

"Why?"

"Just do it."

"Do you know how hard it is to take my eyes off you?"

"I hope it's hard," she purred. "Close your eyes. Don't worry, I won't let you trip over anything. You do trust me, don't you?"

Reluctantly, Daniel obeyed.

Taylor squeezed his hand and walked him forward. He heard the gritty material of the flat roof crunch beneath the soles of his polished black dress shoes, felt the balmy spring breeze on his cheeks.

He knew she had a seduction plan. Taylor loved seducing him and he loved being seduced by her scenarios. He wondered what she had up her sleeve tonight. What was going to take place on that rooftop? He licked his lips, anticipating.

Some might say he was sex-obsessed, but he'd never been that way before. Not even when he was a teenager. He'd always been so focused on his goal. The air force. Becoming a doctor. Following the family tradition of military M.D. set by his grandfather in the M.A.S.H. units of the Korean War and continued by his dad in Vietnam.

And then he'd met Taylor.

They'd made love the night they'd met in the coat closet at the mixer and he'd certainly never done anything like that before.

"I'm a bad girl," she'd whispered in his ear, just before she'd nibbled it. "Are you sure a good soldier like you can handle someone like me?"

"Airman," he'd corrected, and she'd just laughed.

Remembering hardened his dick. Daniel grinned. He'd done far more than handle her, and he wanted to do it again.

"Okay, you can open your eyes," she said and let go of his hand. "Ta-da."

Daniel blinked. There in the middle of the rooftop—in a circle of lighted candles scented with the smell of vanilla—sat a four-poster bed adorned with throw pillows.

"You've conquered ROTC," she said and stepped toward him. "You've reached the top of this world. I'm going to give you the best send-off any second lieutenant heading for medical school at Bethesda ever got."

He was stunned she'd gone to so much trouble for him. "Taylor, how did you—"

"Shh." She laid an index finger against his lips. "No talking. The time for talking has passed."

Daniel growled low in his throat, all primal man, wrapped his arms around her waist and pulled her up tight against him. God, she was so wonderful and he loved her so much. He couldn't begin to describe what he was feeling. He was just going to have to show her.

He kissed her. Hard and hot and frantic. She laughed and the sound shot electricity straight to his dick.

Heedlessly, he grabbed the hem of her dress and pulled the thing over her head.

Taylor gasped and her eyes lit up with delight. She wriggled in his arms, the lace of her pink bra scratching lightly across the muscles of his chest. The strip of her matching pink thong panties stretched against her pale, shaved skin resembled a sassy silk tongue.

She reached for his hat, whisking it from his head, her fingertips grazing his forehead in the process. She hooked the hat on one corner of the four-poster bed, and then she came back to undo the herringbone twill tie knotted at his throat. His pulse throbbed beneath the heat of her palm.

Daniel took a deep, steadying breath and placed his hand over hers. He wanted her. Damn, how he wanted her. But reason was telling him this wasn't the time or the place. He was going to ask her to marry him tonight and he wanted to be in charge of the seduction.

"She's a thunder stealer, that one," his grandfather had said to him the first and only time Daniel had brought Taylor home for dinner. "Don't get too attached. She's too bold and impulsive to make a good military wife."

Yes, she was bold and spontaneous and uninhibited, but those were the qualities he admired most in her. So how could he fault her for being herself?

Daniel could have his pick of women. He knew that. Women loved military men and doctors and he'd inherited the strong Corben jaw and his mother's royal-blue eyes. He'd never had a bit of trouble getting dates. But this was the first time he'd ever been so consumed by a woman. None of them had turned him inside out the way Taylor did.

She was fire and passion and unpredictability and that was damned tempting to a man who lived a regimented life.

"What is it?" she whispered. Her lips were painted a stimulating shade of red.

"I'm taking it from here," he told her, whipping off his jacket and tie and recklessly dropping them to the ground before bending to scoop her into his arms.

The moon was out, fat and round, framing the bed

in a spotlight of white. Taylor smelled exotic—spicy, piquant, striking. There was nothing ordinary or demure about her.

"We don't dislike Taylor," his dad had told him earlier when they'd spied Taylor in the reception-hall crowd. "She's just not the girl for you, son. You two come from completely different worlds."

It was true. He came from a dedicated career military family. She hailed from privileged high society and yet, they fitted together. How could their pairing be a mistake when it felt so right?

Her head was thrown back, her smooth creamy neck exposed, her hair trailing down the side of his forearm as he carried her to the bed. Her body was both firm and soft and totally womanly. One of her breasts rested against his bicep as he arranged her gently on the bed.

He stepped back, his eyes drinking her in. She lowered her eyelids halfway and gave him her naughtiest expression. What the woman could do to him with a simple glance left him speechless.

And what he wouldn't give to be able to capture this special moment. Lock it in a bottle. Seal it in a time capsule. Emotions twisted through him. Joy, pride, lust, excitement.

She positioned herself on her side, the pink thong riding high on her hip. Daniel's gaze honed in on the sleek curve of her hip. She ran a hand through her hair, tousling the long, loose curls. One strand fell across her eye, adding to her sexual mystique.

He stared.

Taylor tucked the errant tendril behind one ear

and batted her eyelashes. Her deep, chocolate-brown gaze snagged his, languid as syrup. "Are you going to stand there all night, doctor? Or are you going to quell my fever?"

Marry me, he should have said.

But the moment wasn't right for the words and the ring was in the pocket of his jacket dropped on the ground several feet away.

He grinned instead. "You are so, so hot."

That's romantic, Corben. Way to set the mood.

This evening wasn't going the way he'd planned. He'd meant to take her to their favorite sneak-away spot at the lake, open a bottle of chilled champagne, get down on one knee and ask her to be his wife for the rest of their lives. But he'd lost control of the situation and now they were up here on the roof of the ROTC building, everything on her terms.

She's an heiress. She's used to getting what she wants when she wants it.

Was that such a bad thing? According to his mother it was, but Daniel saw her daring self-confidence as a good thing. She was so alive, so free, so sure of herself. Being with her made him feel the same way about himself.

Taylor's dark-eyed gaze misted with lust. She flicked out her tongue to lick her lips and Daniel forgot about everything except his driving need to sink deeply into her lush body.

She held out her arms. "Why are you standing way over there?"

Growling, he came toward her.

He had one knee on the bed when she reached up with the flat of her bare foot and pressed it against his chest, halting his progress. The sight of her toes, painted to match her bra and panties shot his desire into overload.

"I'm going to wear you out, lieutenant. The way you've never been worn out before. Are you prepared for that?" Her sultry laugh skipped across his eardrums. Helplessly his dick stiffened against the zipper of his uniform pants, anxious to escape confinement.

"Are *you* prepared for that?" He narrowed his eyes as she curled her toes into his muscles.

"Oh, yeah," she murmured. "I'm making sure our last night is one to remember."

"As if you could forget me," he teased, his eyes locking on to hers, his hand going to his belt buckle as he toed off his shoes.

"What was your name again?" she teased right back.

Immediately he flashed to himself in Washington, D.C., and Taylor here on the UT campus. Surrounded by men. He gulped.

Ask her to marry you now.

She dropped her foot, curled up to a sitting position and reached for his zipper.

Daniel groaned.

"Yeah, baby," she cooed as her fingers tugged down the zipper. "That's my big man."

His gaze slid straight through the cleavage of that pink lace bra. She had such gorgeous tits. Perfect size. Full and round and real, but not too big. Just right. Everything about her was just right. He couldn't help reaching out to cup them at the same second as she jerked his pants down his legs.

Taylor was frantic. A wild thing. Going for his underwear next, ripping it off, and then pulling him down on top of her. He was equally hungry. His mouth seared hers as they dissolved into a tumble of arms and legs on the bed.

The atmosphere on the roof was turgid and ripe with the smell of their desire. He wanted Taylor and he wanted her now. Wanted her every way possible.

She reached around to unhook her bra and she tossed if off the bed before wrapping her long, sexy legs around his waist.

His cock throbbed. Blood galloped through his veins, engorging him hard and hot.

"Wait, wait," she gasped. "Can't forget protection." Seemingly from out of nowhere, Taylor produced a condom and moved to roll it onto him. The entire time she was doing it all he could think was—*gotta have her, gotta have her now.*

When she'd finished, she fell spread-eagled onto the bed and he tumbled atop her, his big body pressing her into the mattress. He took command of her lips, but she was ready and waiting for him. She darted her sly sweet tongue into his mouth, rushing pell-mell past his teeth.

Each stroke drove the heat inside him higher and higher. Temperatures rising. Blood boiling. Brain blazing. And his cock—aw, hell, his cock was an inferno.

Taylor raked her fingers through his freshly clipped military haircut and arched her hips upward, driving him mad with the brush of her nipples beaded tight against his chest. And the sight of her flame-red hair curling down her creamy bare skin—*have mercy.*

He inhaled her womanly fragrance, feminine and enticing and the aroma jettisoned him to a whole new level of arousal. He had to taste her, inhale her, touch every inch of her.

Wetting his lips, he struggled to relish each second, mentally noting what was happening so that when he was in medical school cracking the textbooks, suturing wounds, doing scut work for the residents, he could trot out the memory of this night and replay it over and over. The night he graduated college. The same night that he asked the most exciting woman in the world to marry him.

But she was squeezing him so tightly his control just fried. Taylor's lips parted, supple and impatient, mimicking his every move. She dug her fingertips into his spine, squashing his chest against her breasts.

They were nose to nose, Daniel anchoring her to the bed. He slipped one hand down her inner thigh, searching for her womanly heat, finding out how wet she was for him. Gently, he rubbed his index finger along her soft flesh.

Taylor gasped at his touch and her eyes rounded. "Oooh, Danny Boy," she purred huskily.

He groaned in answer as he found his target and slipped a finger into her.

She shivered and her arousal caused a corresponding shudder inside him.

He inched in another finger. When he found her clit with the tip of his thumb, she moaned at the back of her throat, and pushed against his hand.

"Ah, yeah, that's my Taylor," he whispered. Her responsiveness drove him wild.

"I'm not doing this alone," she managed to say as she nipped at his neck. "I want you to—" she quivered "—come along with me."

"You know I can't resist you," he said, the air suddenly hot as blazes.

"Come," she whispered.

He couldn't hold out any longer. He pushed into her. The minute her hot, moist folds engulfed him he found total bliss.

Her fingers were in his hair and she was rocking against him, chanting his name like a mantra. "Daniel, Daniel, Daniel."

She stopped breathing then. She always held her breath before she had an orgasm.

No, no, it was too fast. He wanted this to last. Daniel slowed down, pulled back. "Not yet, sweetheart."

"Don't be mean." She pursed her bottom lip in a pout.

Grinning, he kissed her forehead, her eyelids, her nose, her cheeks, her chin as she wriggled impatiently beneath him. "You want it?"

"I want it now!"

"You got it." He dropped his feet to the ground, pulled her buttocks to the edge of the mattress. His throbbing cock hovered just outside her moist sex. She spread her thighs apart and he nudged against her entrance.

He looked down at her. At her naked body in the moonlight. Her lips were wet and shiny, her hair tousled, her breasts round and luscious. Damn, but she was the sexiest woman he'd ever known.

Taylor writhed against him. "Get inside me now, lieutenant and that's a direct order."

"Yes, ma'am." He sank into her. Taylor grabbed his ass and pulled him in deeper. They groaned in unison. The heat, the night, the moonlight, the flickering candles. The smell of their combined sex. The headiness of the day. Neither one of them lasted long. A few powerful thrusts and they were both over the edge.

Daniel exploded inside her at the same moment Taylor cried out a deep, throaty pleasure.

Minutes later they lay on the bed in a tangle of arms and legs, sticky with sweat. He was completely sated, totally happy.

A drifty, dozy moment passed, and then Taylor murmured, "Daniel."

"Uh-huh?" He breathed lazily.

"We need to talk." She sounded serious.

Daniel rose up on one elbow. The expression on her face was sad, wistful, troubled. It touched him because he'd never seen his high-spirited, fun-loving Taylor look melancholy. His gut clenched. "What's wrong?"

"I can't begin to tell you how great the last four months have been," she said.

"Same here," he replied, his voice gruff with the emotions pushing at the seams of his heart.

"It's been the best four months of my life."

"Yeah, for me, too."

"And now it's coming to an end."

It was almost impossible, but he tried to stay calm. "It doesn't have to end, Taylor. I don't want it to end and I don't think you do, either."

She laughed, but it was a dry, humorless sound that sliced him wide open. "Don't be silly. It has to end."

"You're wrong."

"Be realistic. You're going away. I'm staying here. Besides, you'll be in medical school. Studying, working eighty hours a week."

"We can make it work."

"Long-distance relationships aren't practical."

Since when was Taylor practical? "We're different," Daniel assured her. "You and I. We're not like everyone else."

A strange expression that he couldn't quite read came over her face. Part longing, part regret, part determination, part something else.

Relief?

Could she actually be relieved he was going away? The thought stung like a slap.

"Face it, Daniel. We're fire and ice. It makes for great sex…" She shook her head. "But it's lousy for relationships."

"What are you talking about?"

"We're too different. You know that and I know it. Most of all, your family knows it. This has been fun. Great fun, in fact, but…"

She was breaking up with him.

It hit him then, a sledgehammer between the eyes. He had an engagement ring in his pocket to slip on her finger and she was breaking up with him.

"We need to get out of this now before either one of us gets hurt," she said.

Too late, too late.

Thunderstruck, he sat up and just stared at her. What then was this sudden stabbing in the center of his chest? Was that the kind of hurt she was talking about?

"Taylor…" He started to say more, to plead his case, but he stopped himself. Dammit, he wasn't going to beg. If she didn't want him, she didn't want him. He was an airman. A doctor in training. He came from a long line of strong, capable men. He wasn't going to let a broken heart fell him. Hell, no.

"This is our last hurrah," she said gently and reached out to lay a hand over his, but her eyes were too shiny, her smile forced. "After tonight, it's over, Daniel. It's for the best and we both know it."

No, no, he didn't know that at all. Yes, they came from different worlds. Yes, his parents disapproved. Probably so did her father.

He hardened his jaw, tightened his hands into fists. "That's really the way you want it?"

Taylor nodded. She was checking her emotions, pulling back, detaching herself. He could see it in the murkiness descending over her intense brown eyes.

"I've got to confess, Daniel, this was never anything more than a good time for me."

She couldn't have hurt him more if she'd taken out a knife and driven it straight through his heart. His limbs felt wooden as he searched for his underwear and pants and somehow managed to jam his legs into them and then lace up his shoes.

"You don't have to leave now," she murmured. "The night is still young."

Was it his imagination or did she sound a little panicky? He searched her face for a clue, but she gave away nothing. "Hoo-effing-rah," he said through clenched teeth as he tightened his belt. "Been nice knowing you, Taylor."

He snatched up his shirt, grabbed his jacket, and snagged his hat from the bed post. Had he not been so mad, so hurt, he might have heard her whisper, "I love you, Danny Boy, with all my heart, but this is the way it's gotta be."

2

Present day

"DOCTOR CORBEN?"

Daniel got to his feet in the waiting area of the Department of Defense Manned Space Flight Support Office at Patrick Air Force Base in Cape Canaveral and smiled at the attractive young staff sergeant sitting behind the reception desk. "Yes?"

She returned his smile with a flirtatious slant of her eyelashes. Had word already gotten out that he and Sandy had broken up? "Colonel Grayson is ready for you."

This is it, the conversation leading to the promotion I've been shooting for my entire career.

From the time he was a kid in short pants listening to his father and grandfather talk about the exciting opportunities for air force doctors, he'd dreamed of going into space as a NASA physician. Making colonel before he was forty was a crucial step in that direction.

Daniel squared his shoulders, perfected his best military-officer stance and stalked into Grayson's office, hoping that he struck the perfect balance between cocky and obedient. Assertive, but eager to follow orders. "You asked to see me, sir?"

"I did." Colonel Cooper Grayson was standing. He pointed at the plain straight-backed chair positioned in front of his sturdy metal desk. "Have a seat, Daniel."

He sat, but the expression on Grayson's face troubled Daniel. It wasn't a congratulations-you're-in-the-running-to-make-colonel look.

"When are you going to ask Sandy to marry you?" the colonel asked.

The minute the words were out of his superior's mouth, Daniel tensed. Was this a fishing expedition? Deeming his worthiness for promotion? It was the one question he dreaded. He knew well enough that in the military you were more likely to get promoted if you were married. The service viewed its airmen as more stable, mature and trustworthy if they had a wedding ring on their finger and a passel of kids to support.

He did not have that advantage going for him.

It wasn't that Daniel didn't want to get married or have children. He did. But becoming a doctor had taken all his focus in his younger years. Then later, once he'd completed his internship and residency and he'd met Sandy, well…

He'd thought about asking her to marry him. They'd been dating for four years. She was smart and pretty and safe and predictable. Her father was a career military man so she understood the life. In theory, she was perfect for him.

But she wasn't Taylor.

The unwanted thought popped into his mind. What the hell was he doing thinking about Taylor Milton? He hadn't seen or heard from her in thirteen years.

Still, that woman had excited him like no other, even

though she'd been completely wrong for him. Sometimes, he wondered if she'd ruined him in regard to other women. But no one could measure up to her verve, her sheer enthusiasm, her exuberant life force.

It's what Sandy had accused. He clenched his jaw, remembering their break up weeks earlier.

"Four years I've spent with you, Daniel. Four years of loving you and waiting for you to love me back." Sandy had paused, taken a deep breath. *"You were only with her for a few months and she put such a spell over you that you can't forget her even after all this time. You're in love with a woman who didn't love you back. And I've been waiting with open arms, aching for you to love me."*

"You're wrong. I'm not still in love with Taylor. I haven't even thought about her in years."

"Maybe not consciously, Daniel, but sometimes you call out her name in your sleep."

He'd blinked. "I do?"

Sandy had nodded, tears spilling from her eyes. "Not often, but you have."

Daniel had felt as if he'd been poleaxed. Was it true? Did he still dream of Taylor? He didn't remember that.

"The thing is, you're holding on to the past, to the ghost of some long-lost love. You can't let go of her and love the real flesh-and-blood woman standing in front of you."

"I do love you, Sandy," he'd said, but the words had sounded false. He did care about her, just not in the way she wanted and needed.

"Not in the way I deserve."

"No," he agreed.

"I know." She'd exhaled audibly.

She'd been right. Damn him, he'd known she was right. "You're breaking my heart here," he'd said as she headed for the door, suitcase in hand.

She'd whirled on him, eyes flashing and dropped her suitcase. "No, Daniel, you're breaking mine. Only love can break a heart and Taylor Milton broke yours years ago. You're damaged goods."

"I'm not," he'd declared hotly. "I've long since moved on."

"Maybe in your head you have." She had stepped across the room toward him, hammered a small fist against the left side of his chest. "But not here, not where it counts, not in your heart."

"Sandy..." Daniel had let his words trail off. What else had there been to say? It hurt to know that he was hurting her, but he couldn't make himself love her, no matter how much he might want to. Was this how Taylor had felt toward him? Pity, guilt, embarrassment? "I'm so sorry for hurting you."

"Physician, heal thyself," Sandy had said, then turned and walked away.

"Well?" Colonel Grayson prompted bringing him back to the present.

"Sandy and I broke up," he said.

"How come?"

"She was pressuring me to get married."

"And you're not ready for marriage?"

"I'm ready, sir," he said, hating the thought that he might lose out on the promotion because he wasn't yet hitched. "But I haven't found the right woman."

"So you're free as a bird. Not dating anyone else?"

"That's correct."

"Hmm," the colonel mused. Daniel had expected his boss to look disappointed, but he did not. "Interesting."

Wariness settled over him. Something was up. "What's this meeting about, sir?"

Grayson clasped his hands behind his back and paced like an agitated jungle cat. "A thorn in my side."

"Excuse me?"

"I've got a thorn in my side and you're the only one I trust to pull it out."

Ah. The colonel had a problem and he perceived Daniel as the solution. That was good news. Solving his superior's issue would go a long way toward proving his worthiness for the promotion.

"Sir." Daniel stood at attention. "How may I be of service to you, sir?"

Grayson stopped pacing and looked over at him. "I like your gung-ho attitude, Corben. Exactly why you're the man for this job."

"What's the assignment? I'm ready to roll up my sleeves and get started."

"You say that now." Grayson gave a rueful laugh. "Wait until you hear what it is."

"Doesn't matter, sir. I'm at your disposal."

Grayson plunked down behind his desk and motioned for Daniel to sit. He did. The Colonel locked on him with a steady gaze. "General Charles Miller came to see me yesterday."

"Yes, sir."

"The general has political aspirations. He's planning on running for public office when he retires at the end of next year. He's eyeing the White House. Sees himself as the next Colin Powell."

"Yes, sir."

"You can drop the 'sir' business, Daniel, it's just you and me in here."

Now Grayson was getting chummy. The thorn in his side must really be throbbing. His curiosity piqued, Daniel leaned forward. "Is this thorn medically related?"

Grayson made a face. "Not exactly."

"Are we dealing under the table here?" Daniel bristled. He'd do anything for his superior as long as it wasn't unethical or against regulations. He was strictly by the book, one of the reasons why he and Taylor had made for such a bad match. She'd been all about breaking the rules.

"No, not really, bending a few rules maybe, but nothing that crosses the line."

"Tell me," Daniel said bluntly.

"Let me just say up front that if you successfully pull off this assignment your promotion is practically a done deal. You'll have my full recommendation to the committee."

"And if I don't?"

Grayson shrugged. "Only twenty-five percent of military officers ever achieve the rank of colonel."

Daniel knew this. He also understood the implication. "I did two tours of duty in a field hospital in the Middle East. I earned a silver star in Afghanistan—"

"And that is the reason why you've made it up the ranks as quickly as you have."

"What do I have to do to make colonel?"

Grayson leaned back in his chair and propped his booted feet on his desk. "One of General Miller's wealthy VIPs has pledged big contribution money if he'll grant a favor."

"Which gets passed down to me."

Grayson nodded. "That's the thorn you'll be pulling out of my side, doctor."

"Lay it on me."

"The general's generous donor wants a backstage pass to our behind-the-scenes action for the next launch of the space shuttle," he said.

"Meaning?"

"She's doing research for—"

"She?"

"That's why I asked you about Sandy. According to the general, his benefactor is young, single, attractive and very rich."

"Ah."

"Anyway, she runs some kind of sex fantasy resort thing and she's in the research stages of planning a new one."

"Like fantasy baseball camp?"

Grayson cleared his throat. "Something like that, except it's for adults. She wants details on test pilots, flight surgeons and astronauts. I don't know the full parameters, I'm sure she'll fill you in."

An ugly tug pulled at the pit of his stomach. "You gotta be kidding me."

His superior officer shrugged, gave him an apologetic look. "I wish I was."

Daniel got to his feet again. "Let me get this straight. You want me to babysit some pampered rich woman who's running around using our high-tech military space program to fuel her little X-rated sexual fantasies?"

"Believe me, Corben. I'm no happier about it than you are. But if we pull this off to her satisfaction, then she'll bankroll Miller's run for the senate. I'll make brigadier general and my job will be open for you to step in."

"How long will she be here?"

"Two weeks."

"Two weeks!"

"A minor inconvenience." Grayson waved a hand, dismissing his objections as if batting away a fly. "The main thing is to keep her out of trouble."

"Trouble?"

His superior officer shifted, looked uncomfortable. "She's got a flamboyant reputation."

Daniel glowered. "How so?"

Grayson shrugged. "General Miller said something about media controversy involving her last project. Again, I don't know the details. But we need to keep a tight lid on her visit."

Daniel blew out his breath, shook his head. "I wish I could help you, sir, but if you recall I'll be in Moron, Spain, next week on launch day running the TAL disaster drill."

"I know. That's the main reason I need you and not anyone else," Grayson said, smiling for the first time since Daniel had come into the room. "First of all, you're discreet. Second, it's the perfect solution. Get her out of the country while seeming to give her what she wants."

"She's going to want to be at the Cape for the Atlantis launch, sir, not at some TAL site."

"Then it's up to you to convince her it's better to be at Moron during the launch than here."

"How am I supposed to do that?"

"You're smart and you can be charming. You figure it out."

"I don't like this," Daniel grumbled.

"But you'll do it?" Grayson's eyes drilled into him.

"Do I have a choice?"

"Depends on how badly you want my job."

Daniel glared. "I've worked damned hard for this promotion. This isn't fair."

"No," Grayson said glibly. "This is the Air Force."

TAYLOR MILTON couldn't stop grinning as she drove her rented silver convertible 911 Turbo Porsche toward Cape Canaveral. General Charles Miller, her late father's best friend since high school, had come through for her in a big way.

Just thinking about how she was going to have access to top-gun pilots, shuttle astronauts and sexy Air Force flight surgeons sent a shiver of delight down her spine. This in-depth research was bound to make her planned fourth fantasy resort—Out of this World Lovemaking—a smashing success.

She turned on the radio, flipped through the stations, caught the refrain from a long-ago song and her fingers froze on the button.

"Unchained Melody."

The song that had been playing at the sixties-themed campus mixer when she and Daniel had first laid eyes on each other.

Their song.

Not terribly original, she supposed. "Unchained Melody" was a lot of people's song, but not among her peer group. The haunting tune jettisoned her back thirteen years.

In her mind's eye, she saw Daniel the way he'd

looked as a newly minted Air Force second lieutenant. Young, earnest and tender, but at the same time, he'd possessed a powerful, commanding presence. Daniel had been tall, muscular, built like a firefighter. Dark hair, startlingly blue eyes, broad shoulders, washboard abs. She wondered if he was still as fit and trim.

He hadn't been at all like any of the other young men she'd dated: reckless, randy, cavorting, out for nothing but a good time. He'd been serious, dedicated, focused and principled. Little had she guessed that the qualities in him she admired the most would spell the end of their love affair.

When she was dreaming up ideas for her new resort, she'd asked herself what it was that she personally found sexy, and a full-on visual of Daniel—and the way he'd looked coming out of his military uniform—had gobsmacked her.

Military men were sexy. Doctors were sexy. Astronauts were sexy. Why not combine all three? Feature military doctors and the test pilots and the astronauts they cared for. Once that idea hit, she knew she had to do her research at Patrick Air Force base and the Kennedy Space Station at Cape Canaveral. Hence the call to her godfather, General Charles Miller, known to her as Uncle Chuck.

Taylor pushed a hand through her wind-tousled hair and took the freeway off ramp. She couldn't stop herself from wondering about Daniel. Had he achieved his dream of becoming a doctor? Was he still in the military? Knowing his family and Daniel's desire to follow in their traditional footsteps, she imagined that was the case.

The memories came flooding back and for a quick second her throat tightened as she thought of how she'd once loved him so desperately. She tasted the memory of their courtship, sweet and rich and intense. A vision of their second date flashed through her mind. He'd taken her to an upscale restaurant he could ill afford simply because he wanted to impress her.

Even now, the endearing gesture made her throat tighten.

The waiter had stashed them into a corner of the candlelit French restaurant. She'd found a small bouquet of red-and-white spider lilies on the linen-draped table, sweetening the air with an anise-scented prickle. He'd ordered for them both, choosing fennel-scented crab cake appetizers and filet mignon with duchess potatoes for the main meal.

Funny, she could still remember that meal and she couldn't remember what she'd had for dinner the night before.

Their hands had brushed as they'd both reached for the bread basket filled with yeasty multi-grain rolls. He'd stared into her eyes, filling her with molten heat. That look had cinched the deal. She was hungry and for far more than food.

For dessert, they'd shared an oozy chocolate soufflé with Obuse wine, a wickedly delicious dessert port recommended by the wine steward. It was only then that she learned he rarely drank alcohol and he'd quickly gotten tipsy on chocolate and Obuse. She'd taken his keys, driven him back to his apartment and stayed the night.

Quickly, she batted the thoughts away. Not love, no. Just the ridiculous infatuation of a college girl.

She remembered how he'd kissed her that evening. Hard and passionate, full of yearning and desire. Daniel had kissed the way heroes kissed in the old movies her father loved. Humphrey Bogart and Ingrid Bergman. Clark Gable and Vivian Leigh. Burt Lancaster and Deborah Kerr.

Movies from a bygone era had been her main connection to her father. At least in the early years, before his commuter airline—Milton Air—had grown to consume all his time. "I work so much because I love you so much," he'd told her. "It's all for you." She supposed it was where she'd gotten her flair for the dramatic, her love of daydreams and fantasies.

"This was the golden age of filmmaking," her father would tell her, when she was a little girl in pigtails. She'd snuggle up in his lap in the private screening room he'd built in their home back before such things were popular among people who could afford them. Her father's valet, Mr. McGulicutty would thread the film projector, and Agnes, the cook would make buttered popcorn. "*Casablanca* was your mother's favorite movie."

Her mother had died giving birth to her at age forty-two. Her father had been just shy of fifty. Bringing Taylor into the world had cost Lily Milton her life. But her father had never once made her feel as if she was to blame. Taylor, however, couldn't escape the knowledge that by being born she'd caused her mother's death.

"Why couldn't Rick and Elsa be together, Daddy?" she always asked at the end of *Casablanca*. "They loved each other so much."

"That's exactly why they couldn't be together," he'd

say. Then he would kiss the top of her head and get a faraway look in his eyes. "When you love that deeply, you'll sacrifice for the other person's happiness. Even if it means that you have to be unhappy. That's real love, when you can let go of your loved ones so they can be what they need to be."

It was only years later, after her father had died, that Taylor found her mother's journal in his safe-deposit box and learned that her father had never wanted her mother to get pregnant. Lillian Milton been a brittle diabetic and doctors had warned she might not survive a pregnancy. But her mother had wanted a baby so badly and her father had loved her mother so much, he'd agreed to let her try. And in the process of letting her be what she needed to be, he'd lost her forever.

"You always lose the one you love, Taylor," her father used to say. "Never forget that. You lose them. One way or another. Always."

Silly. Fanciful. Thinking about the past. Taylor blinked back the tears that had formed along her eyelashes.

Thankfully, she heard her cell phone ring, distracting her from the sad memories. She flipped it open. "Speak to me," she said to her executive assistant Heather Rheiss.

"The Italian resort had another incident."

"What now?" Her third destination fantasy resort in Venice, featuring "Make Love Like a Courtesan" and its masculine counterpart, "Make Love Like Casanova" had been the target of several disturbing occurrences.

First off, malfunctioning smoke alarms had allowed a fire in the laundry room to go undetected until it had done several thousand dollars' worth of damage. It was suspicious, because the smoke alarms had just passed inspection the week before.

Then, after one of the scheduled banquet feasts, several resort guests contracted food poisoning and had to be sent to the hospital for treatment.

And finally, the thing that had drawn her to Venice to check things out for herself; a Renoir was stolen from the resort because the security system had been turned off. The police suspected an inside job. She'd fired the manager, hired someone new and stayed a week to show them the ropes. The police had no leads in the theft and she'd filed an insurance claim.

Taken one by one, all the incidents seemed unconnected, but together, Taylor was starting to see a pattern. Was someone trying to undermine her resorts? She was no stranger to controversy. Outspoken religious fundamentalists denigrated her resorts and condemned them as hedonistic and wicked. Kinky customers threatened to sue because they thought Eros Air should fulfill their illegal fantasies. Competitors were jealous of the way she'd taken stodgy Milton Airlines and given it a stunning new makeover in the form of Eros Air. It was all part of doing business in the tourism industry.

"The new manager you hired caught an undercover exposé reporter posing as a guest."

Taylor groaned. "I don't have time for this."

"Don't worry, it's been handled. The manager confiscated the photos he'd taken and threw the reporter out on his ear. I just thought you should know."

"Thanks, Heather. I appreciate the heads up."

"No problem. Where are you now?"

"I'm almost at the air base. I'll check in with you later."

"I'll be holding down the fort."

Taylor closed her phone and followed the signs to the main entrance of the air base and stopped at the front gate.

"Name?" asked the security officer.

Pushing her designer sunglasses up higher on her nose with a freshly manicured fingernail, she gave him her most winsome smile. "Taylor Milton," she said. "Colonel Grayson is expecting me."

"Yes, ma'am." He nodded. "General Miller ordered an escort to be waiting for you."

"How kind of him," she said.

"Just follow that jeep." The security officer nodded at the vehicle that waited on the other side of the gate with the engine chugging. "He'll take you where you need to be."

"Thank you so much." She wriggled her fingers goodbye as the airman raised the gate arm to let her pass.

The jeep led her through the Air Force base, past rows of tidy, spick-and-span, no-frills structures. The military had been a perfect fit for Daniel. His personality matched service life—straightforward, precise, no tolerance for anything or anyone who did not toe the organizational line. No wonder their relationship had crashed and burned. She was complicated, freewheeling, a true maverick. It was those traits that had made her such a success in the cutthroat airline industry. She did not play follow the leader very well.

In fact, when she saw the lettering on the building where she knew she was expected, she blew around the jeep with a wave of her hand and a brilliant smile for the startled young staff sergeant behind the wheel.

"Ciao," she called out to the solider on her way

past, still in Venice mode. "I can find my way from here, thanks."

"Ma'am, ma'am, you need an escort!" he hollered, but she kept right on going. Rules were for military personnel. Not her.

She zoomed ahead, pulling into Colonel Grayson's parking space in front of the administration building.

The young sergeant stopped his jeep behind her and came running over to her convertible. His face was flushed and he looked flustered. "Ma'am, this is a military base."

"I'm aware of that." She grabbed her purse, got out and gave him a dazzling smile.

"You can't park here," he said weakly. "It's reserved for Colonel Grayson."

"I'm sure he won't mind. Where is he, by the way? I'm supposed to have a meeting with him."

"N-n-no, ma'am," the poor sergeant stammered.

"No?"

He shook his head and his face paled. Instantly, she felt sorry for him. Poor guy was probably terrified he'd have to pay the price because she didn't follow the rules. She'd make sure to mention to the colonel that any violations were completely her responsibility. The young man shouldn't be held accountable for her actions.

"Colonel Grayson's not on the base this morning, ma'am. You've been reassigned to our second-in-command."

"He's passing me off?" she said it lightly, but she was irritated. Uncle Chuck had assured her she would have an audience with the base commander.

"I…he's…"

"I'm the one who's stuck babysitting the spoiled princess," growled an arrogant voice from behind her.

Taylor spun around, ready to deliver a tongue-lashing to the insolent man who'd interrupted her, but the second she laid eyes on him all the air left her body.

Daniel Corben.

Looking just as disturbed to see her as she was to see him.

3

RECOGNITION knifed Daniel in the chest.

It couldn't be, but the hell if it wasn't.

The very woman who'd sledgehammered his heart thirteen years ago which had led to his break-up with Sandy now.

"Daniel," Taylor said, her voice low, husky. She cleared her throat, slipped off her sunglasses and took him in. He spied the nervousness in her eyes as she inspected the insignias on the collar of his uniform shirt before lifting her defiant chin. "Lieutenant-Colonel Dr. Daniel Corben, I see."

His heart thumped and his palms slicked as he peered into those familiar brown eyes. Taylor Milton in the flesh and looking far more beautiful than any woman had the right to look.

Twin dots of color pinked her cheeks and he felt a corresponding heat rise inside him. Slowly, he raked his gaze over her, starting with her gorgeous red hair, now stylishly streaked with blond threads. He couldn't help but lust after her swan-like throat and then the swell of her breasts, before rolling right on down to those long, shapely legs. He remembered exactly what it felt like to have those legs wrapped tightly around him in the throes of passion.

Something ripped loose inside his chest, a tearing-away sensation. God, she was gorgeous. The years had been generous to her. In fact, she'd grown even lovelier with the passing of time. He shook his head, tried to shake off the attraction. But it was useless.

"I should have known," Daniel said, dragging his gaze back to her face.

"Known?" she echoed, seeming confused.

"*You're* the one who wrapped General Miller around your little finger. Bravo, Taylor. You've always had a knack for bringing men to their knees." His tone came out harsher than he had intended.

Her eyes widened as if he'd slapped her, and he immediately felt like a jerk. She moistened her lips, swallowed. "You're upset with me."

"Yeah," he admitted. "I am."

She shifted her weight, but held his gaze. "Why?"

"Because you're intent on making a mockery of the thing I love most."

Her eyes darkened. "The Air Force."

"I want you to know I'm adamantly opposed to the reason you're here."

"Duly noted," she said coolly.

As coolly as when she'd told him that their love affair had been nothing more than a fun fling. It had been thirteen years. The memory shouldn't still sting.

But it did.

"I tried to tell her, sir," the anxious young staff sergeant was saying, "that she couldn't just barge in. There's protocol. This is a military base. But she wouldn't listen to me. I—"

Daniel held up a hand to silence the kid, who was

about the same age Daniel had been when he'd graduated college. Not once did he take his eyes off Taylor. "I've got it from here, Staff Sergeant. You're dismissed."

"Thank you, sir." The young man snapped off a salute.

"Impressive." Taylor lifted an eyebrow. Mocking him?

Daniel narrowed his gaze, his world condensing to her. Just Taylor and no one else. He could no longer see the staff sergeant hustling around to his jeep, although he could hear the young man's shoes slapping quickly against the asphalt.

She boldly held his stare, but Daniel could see past the bravado in the way she slipped her fingers through her hair, trying to tame the windblown strands. He remembered she had a habit of running her hand through her hair when she was nervous. Nice to see that some things didn't change.

Her chest moved with each breath of air. Her magnificent breasts strained the buttons of the expensive yellow silk blouse she wore. He thought of her nipples, recalled how sweet they'd tasted. With her sun-streaked red hair, Taylor looked damned delicious in yellow. Like marigolds in a wheat field.

Her fingers dropped from her hair in one long graceful movement and fell to the pocket of her sleek charcoal-gray slacks. Her fingernails, he noted, sported a flawless French manicure.

Daniel wondered, not for the first time, how he'd ever ended up with a woman like her even for a little while. She was pure class from the top of her head to the tips of her pedicured toes peeping from golden high-heeled sandals. She came from money, privilege. He was military all the way. An officer first, a doctor second.

His eyes latched on to her lips. Full, lavish, painted the color of the pink Gerbera daisies he'd given his mom the other day. He held his breath.

Waiting.

What was he waiting for?

Taylor took a thick tortoise-shell hairclip from the gold pocketbook that matched her designer sandals, pulled back several long strands of hair with one hand and anchored them in place with the clip. The remaining hair, not caught up in the barrette, fell in soft, sexy waves about her face.

Her languid movements stirred up her scent, bringing her perfume to him. Honeysuckle. The sweet farm-girl scent was in total opposition to the sleek reality. Urban, hip, on-top-of-the world. Creator of sexual-fantasy resorts.

The morning sun peeped behind a cloud, cloaking her face one half in shadow, the other in light, illuminating the dichotomy that was Taylor Milton. On the one hand constant, on the other enigmatic and changeable. Daniel peered into her eyes, glimpsing something melancholy lurking there.

Old memories, heartfelt feelings—both happy and sorrowful—shimmered between them like heat waves off asphalt, thin, fragile, elusive as snow in the desert.

A chord was struck, only for a whisper of a second. But it was enough to pull the breath from their lungs in a synchronized exhale.

He focused on her mouth. A mouth he yearned to kiss. A mouth that still called to him in the dark recesses of dreams he hadn't known he'd dreamed. He moved toward her. Not thinking, just longing, craving, *wanting*.

She didn't step back.

Daniel never took his eyes off her face. It felt so natural for him to kiss her. To pull her into his arms, rekindle their past, fan the sparks, make a new one.

He stepped forward, closing the small gap. All at once, he realized their lips were almost touching. She didn't flinch. She seemed as mesmerized as he.

Knock it off, Corben, this is completely unprofessional.

And yet he couldn't seem to stop himself. He didn't want to stop himself. What was he trying to prove? That he could intimidate her?

Not cool.

Daniel thought he'd grown beyond his resentment over the way Taylor had broken things off with him. He was disturbed to discover he had not. He thought of himself as a rational man, but around her, he felt…what did he feel? Irrational? Fevered? Out of control?

A miserable combination of all three, he concluded.

For the first time, he fully understood why his parents hadn't liked her. Taylor didn't play by the rules and both medicine and the military were all about rules. She was rebellious and opinionated and imaginative and creative. She blazed her path and didn't care what anyone thought.

And the hell of it was Daniel had loved her for all those things.

The heat of her skin radiated outward, zapped into him. It was all he could do not to act on his impulses and take her right there in the parking lot.

She flicked out her tongue, tracing the pink tip over her moist lips. He knew it was an innocent gesture born of nervousness, but it had the same effect as if it had been carefully calculated. His gut squeezed and his cock hardened. The unexpectedness of his desires scared the hell out of him. Like it or not, he still cared for her.

Dammit. He did not want to care for her. He could not. Should not. Would not.

Her eyes widened again and she tucked her elbows close to her sides. Suddenly, she looked utterly vulnerable. As if she would shatter like fragile glass if he were to touch her. Daniel could read his own fears reflected in her eyes. They were both unsettled by a chemistry that time had not erased.

They stared into each other with a mix of stunned surprise, affection and stark sexual need.

It was still there. The old flare. The embers just waiting to be stoked. All this time and he still burned for her in a way that shook him to his core.

Fate had brought them back together again.

Reunited them.

Reunited.

The idea felt both wonderful and treacherous. Wonderful because there was the hint of hope, treacherous because it was all an illusion. A pang of longing pierced him.

That's when Daniel knew that his promotion was in serious jeopardy.

"So you're my escort," Taylor said with all the cool aplomb and calm control she could muster, hiding the fact that inside she was a quivering mass of nerves and anxiety.

"Feels like old times, huh?" Daniel said, his voice loaded with sarcasm.

One look at him and she was jettisoned back thirteen

years. With the passing of time, she'd told herself she'd embellished their attraction. That it was nothing more than the fuzzy sweet memory of a love that used to be. But here, now, feeling the raw, aching chemistry again, she realized she'd actually downplayed it.

What was she going to do?

She'd never bargained on running across him, on feeling like this; for a split second she thought perhaps Uncle Chuck was playing matchmaker, hooking her up with her old college sweetheart. Then she remembered that General Miller knew nothing about her youthful affair with Daniel. She'd never even told her father of their liaison because it had been too new, too romantic to share with a man who viewed love as something that had to be sacrificed. This hook-up was sheer, miserable bad luck.

Or destiny, whispered a voice in the back of her mind.

"It's my duty to show you around," he replied.

She could tell from the sharp-edged light in his eyes and his pointed tone of voice that *duty* was not the word he really wanted to use. The military had disciplined him to hold his tongue. Not that he'd ever been great at expressing his feelings. Typical strong, silent type.

But Taylor was a Milton born and bred. She could hide her real emotions just as well as he could. It was the one thing they had in common.

But hiding her feelings took a toll.

What she yearned to do was fling herself into his arms, tell him just how stupid she'd been to send him away all those years ago. Of course, she didn't do that, instead, she called him on it. "You disapprove of my being here."

"Patrick is a restricted military base."

"Aren't all military bases restricted?"

"Civilians shouldn't be allowed to go running around unchecked." His chin hardened.

"Correct me if I'm wrong, but I'm checked. You're here to check me."

"You're here because you're throwing money at General Miller's political campaign, that's it."

"And that's bad because…?"

"Not everyone has your wealth and privilege. Not everyone has pockets big enough to support their whims."

That irritated her. "My business is not a whim."

He said nothing, just scrutinized her with those stalwart blue eyes that shook her up.

Taylor forced a smile. She refused to let him rattle her. "So, tell me all about Lieutenant Colonel Dr. Daniel Corben. I'm assuming you're married. Got a big brood of kids."

"No wife, no children." Daniel shook his head and her foolish, foolish heart soared.

"Oh," she said, struggling to sound neutral, as if she didn't care. But damn if she didn't sound hopeful to her own ears. She felt hopeful, too. Why should she be hopeful when he'd made it clear he didn't want her here?

Stop it. There's a good reason you broke up with him.

But for the life of her—in that moment as her eyes drank him in—she couldn't remember what it was, why she'd lied to him and told him their love affair had been nothing more than a fling. Why she'd walked away from the best thing that had ever happened to her.

Pulse pounding, she searched his face. The years had been lavishly generous. Maturity had deepened his good looks, ripening his masculine appeal. He was bigger than she remembered. Taller, harder. He'd been handsome before, but now…?

Now, he was *extraordinary.*

His shoulders had broadened and so had his muscular thighs and biceps. His posture was ramrod-straight, his presence commanding. He wore a white lab jacket over his basic uniform. His face was attractively fuller, less rangy than it had been, but his waist was just as narrow. His hair was a bit longer than the buzz cut he'd had for military induction, but it was still quite short and tidy. She couldn't spy even a hint of gray.

And his eyes. His devastatingly gorgeous eyes were as impossibly blue as ever.

"How about you?" he asked.

"What?" She blinked.

"Is there a Mr. Milton? Any little Taylors running around?"

"Me?" Taylor laughed, desperate to appear casual and unaffected by this strange turn of events. How could she still be affected by him after all these years? "Not hardly."

"It's a fair question. You're thirty-three now. No ticking biological clock?"

"That's not any of your business." The answer was yes. She did think about kids. Especially since her father had died, since she was all alone in the world, but she didn't have to tell him that.

"So you've never been married?"

"No."

"Boyfriend?"

"Not currently. You know me." She laughed again, trying to sound carefree. "I'm not the kind to settle down."

"Still all about fun, fun, fun, huh?" He said *fun* as though it was a dirty word.

"I do enjoy a good time." She battered her eyelashes in a facetious gesture.

He frowned. "I know."

Her pulse quickened. "I never made a secret of it."

"I never said you did."

If you only knew how much it hurt me to have to hurt you...

She stifled the urge to jump into her Porsche and zoom away from the intensity of those snapping blue eyes. Eyes that seemed to possess a hidden meaning all their own. At the same time an equally compelling impulse had her wanting to kiss him with a fervency born of urgent familiarity.

But she did neither.

Thirty-three years as the only child of a billionaire airline executive had honed her ability to cloak her true feelings behind a happy-go-lucky facade. The skill had given her the strength to send Daniel away on the night of his graduation. From the looks of him now— disciplined, a doctor, a lieutenant colonel involved with the aerospace program—it had been the right decision. He had achieved all his dreams because she'd let him go.

Taylor took a deep breath, steeling herself. She could handle this.

And yet, the intensity of those blue eyes unsettled her in a way nothing else could.

"I remember a lot of things about you," he added.

The criticism in his voice grabbed her in a stranglehold. She knew she'd hurt him, yes, but she'd been hurt, too. That part he didn't understand. He stood looking at her, his expression a combination of judgment and annoyance.

"You haven't changed a bit, Taylor," Daniel said. "Still beautiful and as inaccessible as ever."

"I…I've changed," she said, denying his accusation.

"Yeah?" He arched an eyebrow. "How's that?"

I learned how to live without you.

Taylor drew herself up tall. "I'm running my father's airline now," she answered. "I've overhauled it completely and we're more successful than ever."

"How is your father?"

"Dad passed away four years ago."

"Taylor, I…I'm so sorry." He reached out a hand, but seemed to think better of it, and let his arm fall to his side. "I know he was your only family. That must have been so hard on you."

His sympathy pushed a lump of unshed tears into her throat. "I managed."

Casually, she slipped her sunglasses on, trying her best not to let him see that her hands were trembling, hiding her eyes behind the barrier of UV lenses. Perspiration dewed her upper lip. Not so much from the warm morning sun as from his unwavering gaze.

At that moment, a young airman came running up to them. "Doctor Corben, Doctor Corben!"

"What is it, airman?" Daniel's voice was authoritative, commanding. A shiver tripped down Taylor's spine at the sound of it.

"We've got…there's been…" The young man was hyperventilating.

Daniel rested a hand on his shoulder. "Slow down. Take a deep breath."

"I…it's an emergency, hurry, hurry."

Alarm lifted the hairs on Taylor's arm. She'd never been any good during emergencies.

"Where?" Daniel's expression was calm and assertive.

"Motor pool…" the guy wheezed out. "My buddy Mac. Vehicle jack collapsed. Got him pinned underneath a Jeep. He can't breathe. There's blood."

"Let's go." Daniel and the airman took off at a sprint.

"What do I do?" Taylor called.

"You wanted in on the action," Daniel barked over his shoulder. "Come on."

Taylor followed them, but had trouble keeping up in her high-heeled sandals. Finally, she stopped, peeled them off and ran after them, the straps of her shoes looped around her fingers.

Daniel and the airman entered the hanger building housing military vehicles out of service for repairs. The smell of oil and diesel fuel burned her nose. Vehicle parts were strewn around, as well as various tools that looked as if they'd been dropped in a hurry. A stack of tires initially blocked her view, but as she rounded the corner she saw a cluster of airmen hovered around a Jeep.

The minute they saw Daniel, the airmen immediately parted as if he was Moses and they were the Red Sea.

"Thank God, you're here, Doc," said a senior airman with relief in his voice. "We knew better than to try to get the Jeep off him, even though he was begging us."

"Good job." Swiftly, Daniel knelt beside a pair of uniformed legs protruding from underneath the vehicle. As the men related what had happened, Taylor could hear the victim moaning softly.

Daniel issued orders and the airmen leapt into action. They scrambled here and there; one airman going for a first aid kit, a second one bringing in a hydraulic lift, another rushing out to wait for the medics to arrive.

The coppery taste of adrenaline spilled into her mouth as she watched the scenario unfold. In a matter of minutes, they had the vehicle off the victim. Daniel sprang into action with skills that took her breath away. His assured self-confidence was amazing.

Taylor watched, agog. Sure, she knew he was a doctor, but knowing it intellectually and seeing him in action as a strong, decisive leader whose actions saved lives, were two different things. The boy she'd once known had become a powerful, influential man.

Ambulance sirens screamed to a halt outside the hangar door and two medics hustled in to load the victim onto the gurney. They'd brought a portable cardiac monitor with them and Daniel slapped the leads onto the man's chest, busily barking out instructions about IV solutions and pain medication and other medical stuff Taylor didn't understand.

The medics carried out his orders, seemingly doing a dozen things at once at the same time they were wheeling the victim toward the ambulance.

"You riding with us, Doc?" one of the medics asked.

Daniel's head came up then, his eyes meeting Taylor's and she realized he'd completely forgotten about her until that moment. She stood there barefooted, holding her five-hundred-dollar sandals, as a gaggle of airmen ogled her. She felt distinctly out of place.

"We'll meet you there."

We. He was taking her with him.

The ambulance raced off and Daniel commandeered a Jeep that was parked outside the hangar. "Get in," he said.

She climbed in beside him, slipping on her shoes as he drove. Her pulse pounded in her temples, her head spun, overwhelmed by what she'd just witnessed.

"I thought you were a flight surgeon to the astronauts," she said.

"I am, but that doesn't mean I don't respond to emergencies."

"I didn't mean that," she corrected. "Of course you'd respond to any emergency. I did some research before coming here and I was surprised to learn a flight surgeon isn't really a surgeon. It's just what they call the doctors who take care of the flight team."

"I'm an actual surgeon as well. Trained in a field hospital in Iraq."

"Oh, I didn't know."

"Why would you?"

"So you won't be following this airman's case?"

"No, I'm just going along to make sure everyone is okay and to brief the physician who'll be taking over his care."

"I see. How severe are the man's injuries?"

"When the jack collapsed, the Jeep fell on his chest."

Taylor hissed in a breath.

"He would have been crushed to death if he hadn't been wearing a special protective vest. There was a group of us instrumental in getting a policy passed that required mechanics to wear them when working underneath vehicles."

"So your administrative measures saved a life."

He turned his head, a smile of pure triumphant pride on his face. "It seems so."

"That's amazing."

Ahead of them the ambulance pulled into the emergency entrance of the base hospital. Daniel parked the Jeep in the parking lot and hopped out. Taylor rushed to keep up with him. He stalked into the emergency room, following the medics and barking more orders to the hospital staff.

They converged on the patient.

Once the emergency-room physician appeared and Daniel had briefed him on the accident, he turned to Taylor. "We've got to go back to the hangar, find out exactly what happened and file an incident report."

"Okay." The morning's events left her out of breath and at a loss for words.

Daniel spent the next half hour interviewing the airmen in the motor pool and then he led her to his office while he wrote up his report.

Taylor took the opportunity to jot down a few notes of her own and she was surprised to find her hands trembled as she wrote, the morning's excitement extracting a toll on her nerves. Her admiration for Daniel's supreme cool in a crisis shot her respect for him into the stratosphere.

Straightening in her seat, she sneaked a glace at him and her skin immediately tingled. Daniel was watching her and the expression in his mesmerizing blue eyes was one of pure longing.

4

DANIEL hadn't expected to feel such craving.

It bothered him.

The craving.

He didn't want the feeling, but there it was, burning bright and hot and insistent. Two hours ago his life had been his own. But the second he'd set eyes on Taylor, insanity ruled. Rational thought flew from his head. His reasoning that he valued so highly, fled. One look and he was consumed with a lust far more potent than anything he'd ever felt before—including the very first time they'd met—and it was all focused on her. He was shackled by an all-consuming desire to mate.

With her and only her.

Even now, sitting here across from her in his office he couldn't stop his gaze from seeking her out, couldn't believe the powerful sizzle as he drank her in with his eyes.

Taylor's eyes widened and she rubbed her bare arms as if suddenly chilled. "Are you going to stare at me all day?" she asked lightly. "Or are you going to show me around?"

Just get this over with. Get her out of here. Get back to your life.

Daniel grunted, struggling to keep his desire off his face. He got to his feet. "Come on, Brick, let's roll."

DANIEL had called her Brick.

The whole time they were touring the Kennedy Space Center, Taylor could think of nothing else.

Had it been an accidental slip of the tongue for him to use the nickname he'd given her on the night that they'd first met? Or had it been intentional? And if it had been intentional, why had he used the moniker?

Daniel had called her by the silly college nickname he'd bestowed upon her.

It was their private inside joke. The first time they'd met at that campus mixer, Daniel had walked up, given her a besotted grin and clutched his head.

"What's wrong?" she'd asked, immediately concerned.

"Has someone being doing construction around here?"

"What?" Taylor had blinked, not understanding what he was getting at.

"Because just one look at you and I feel like I've just been hit by a ton of bricks."

She'd laughed. She hadn't been able to help herself. He'd seemed so earnest and more than a little vulnerable, shifting his weight and looking sheepish that he was even saying something so goofy.

He'd claimed the comment wasn't a line, that he'd never used it before. He swore the glib phrase had sprung spontaneously from his lips the minute he'd slapped eyes on her. She really hadn't believed him, but it had made her smile, so he'd kept using the nickname and whenever anyone had asked about it, he refused to tell them. "That's our little secret," he would say shyly and then wink at her.

The space center was crowded with visitors and they'd joined the group listening to the tour guide only to find themselves jostled together. Frequently, Daniel's arm would brush against her shoulder or her hip would collide with his. It shouldn't have been any big deal, but it was. Every tiny bump and touch revved up her body with adrenaline.

She kept sneaking surreptitious glances his way, trying to gauge whether their contact was having any effect on him, but the guy was a like a slab of marble— stony, immovable, at least when it came to his emotions.

Nothing shook him.

Too bad she couldn't say the same.

Sexual awareness caused her body to dampen in a wholly feminine way.

Stop it.

"Too bad we couldn't have come here when we were dating. What with all the talk of rockets and thrust and powerful boosters, we could have slipped off some- where and really enjoyed ourselves." She wriggled her eyebrows suggestively.

"Behave," Daniel commanded, but she could detect a slight lift to his lips as he fought back a smile. "Security cameras are posted everywhere."

"Oh, yeah, like you didn't have fun that time we toured the Texas State Capitol and got thrown out for making out in the Governor's Mansion," she teased.

"We weren't making out, we were just necking."

"You had your hand up my blouse. That classifies as second base, buddy."

He couldn't hold back the grin. "That was a helluva day."

"Incredible," she agreed.

Then they both fell silent, remembering. She could tell that he was thinking about the details of that steamy tryst. Taylor felt her cheeks heat as a warm, sappy sensation brought on by memories and Daniel's proximity liquefied her bones.

"Why don't we head over to the NASA research center and I'll give you a private tour," he offered. "Bypass the crowd."

The way he said *private tour* made her toes curl.

Stop it. Stop it.

"Sounds like a plan." The heel of one of her stilettos teetered on the steps leading down to the exit door.

"Oops, watch your step." He reached out, grabbed her elbow and tucked her against his side.

This close and she could smell him, all soapy clean and serious. Encounter. His scent.

"Those aren't sensible walking shoes," he commented.

"No," she agreed, "but when have I ever been sensible?"

"Point taken." He chuckled, but he didn't let go of her as he guided her down the stairs, out the door and escorted her around to the passenger side of the Air Force jeep.

A few minutes later, they arrived at the NASA research center. Daniel took her inside to give her a glimpse of the future of aerospace travel.

"The vision for space exploration includes destinations far beyond the moon," Daniel told her. "Our latest project is deepening our understanding of artificial gravity. We're studying the stresses that space flight imposes on cardiovascular performance, bone density and neurological functions. We're searching for ways to counter the physiologic effects of extended weightlessness. Come on, I'll show you the short-radius human centrifuge."

"Sounds intriguing."

He crooked his finger and led her into a control room where five technicians wearing headsets were seated at a bank of computers. A woman who appeared to be in charge of the project stood behind the technicians, analyzing the data on their computer screens. Other complicated-looking equipment crowded the room, along with gauges and switches lining a panel beside the computers.

"Good morning, Dr. Corben," the forty-something woman greeted them and there was no mistaking the way her eyes lit up. She liked Daniel. She liked him a lot.

Jealousy, quick as lightning, forked through Taylor. She stepped a little closer to Daniel.

"Hi, Margene. This is Taylor Milton, I'm giving her the VIP tour," he said.

"I don't have her on my list." Margene frowned.

"General Miller authorized her visit."

"Oh, okay. Well, then we need to get you a pass." Margene went to a desk in the corner, pulled out a drawer and tossed a plastic identification tag that read Visitor to Daniel.

He took it and turned to clip it on Taylor's collar. He had to flick a strand of her hair away as he leaned in, the warmth of his breath fanning her cheek and stoking the heat that had been simmering inside her all morning.

"There we go," he said, then stepped away. It wasn't her imagination, his face looked flushed.

"You have impeccable timing, Daniel," Margene purred. "We were just about to run Major Ben Purvis through his first test. You can take your guest into the observation area."

"My name's Taylor," she remarked pointedly.

Daniel put an arm around her shoulder and drew her into a small observation room adjacent to the control room. "Down, Tiger," he murmured. "Margene is a coworker, nothing more."

"As if I care."

"You care." He smirked. "You're jealous."

"That's ridiculous. How can I be jealous? You and me…there's nothing."

"Right." His smile vanished. "And there's nothing between me and Margene."

"She's still rude." -

"She's a research scientist. They're not known for their people skills."

"Hmph, if she worked for me, I'd fire her."

"This isn't the tourism industry, Brick." He'd done it again. He'd called her by that asinine, but heart-torquing nickname. "Now direct your attention to the short-radius centrifuge."

She turned to peer through the observation window into a white, hexagonal room. It was completely empty except for a contraption that looked similar to a carnival Tilt-a-Whirl.

A man in a blue helmet and NASA coveralls was strapped into one side of the gravitational platform of the double-armed centrifuge.

"Let me explain what this experiment is all about," Daniel began. "Right now, even though NASA is working on a prototype spaceship that could carry the astronauts to Mars in three months, the human body can't withstand the effects of antigravity that long. In space, the pull doesn't exist."

"Hmm," she said lightly and wondered whether if they were in space together would she no longer feel this tight tug of attraction between them.

"Muscles atrophy and bones decalcify. The heart shrinks."

"Knots up tiny, huh?"

"Exactly. No pull, no heart, no life. Human frailty remains the primary stumbling block to prolonged space travel."

"So how does spinning someone around in a centrifuge help?" she asked.

"The theory is that if long-term exposure to microgravity makes humans weak, then hypergravity should have the opposite effect. If this proves to be true over a prolonged study, then spaceships can be equipped with hypergravity chambers and the astronauts will be healthy upon their arrival at the moon."

Taylor's eyes never strayed from his face. He looked so animated, so passionate while he was talking about this stuff.

"Since Major Purvis has just started the test group," Daniel explained, "we're first going to monitor his tolerance to see how much gravitational force he can bear."

"You're involved in this study?"

"I'm one of the doctors on the team, yes."

She heard the pride in his voice. He deserved to be proud of his accomplishments. He was one in a million, her Daniel.

He's not your Daniel. You let him go so he could be who he needed to be.

"There are electrodes hooked up to Major Purvis's chest, neck and left wrist, feeding his vital signs into the wires laced through the singlet he's wearing underneath a canvas harness," Daniel went on.

"Have you ever been in the centrifuge?" she asked, cocking her head to study the human lab rat. "You know, so you can understand what the test subjects are experiencing?"

"I can't."

"Why not?"

"Chamber's too small, I'm too tall. But I've interviewed all of the test subjects."

"Tell me about it," she said, enthralled and whipped out her notebook again. She wanted to capture the essence of the aerospace experience to use in her resort. "What's it like?"

"I'll give you a play-by-play as we watch Major Purvis."

"Interesting."

"See where they've shaved that patch of skin above his right temple?" Daniel leaned closer to her.

"Uh-huh."

"That's a Doppler sensor. It measures the velocity of blood flow to his brain. Each time his heart squeezes blood past the sensor, one of the control-room speakers will emit a slurpy noise. Like someone sucking through a straw and hitting the bottom of their milkshake."

"That has to be annoying."

He laughed. "It is."

"So tell me, if your test subject was in a state of sexual arousal and the blood from his brain was descending to other parts of his anatomy, would that affect the sensor?"

"Taylor Milton, what kind of question is that?"

She could tell she'd shocked him. "What?" She grinned impishly. "It's a legitimate question."

"We're not studying the effects of weightlessness on erections," he said.

"Why not?"

"We're going into outer space, not making a porn movie."

"You said the point was to study the physiological effects, well, you don't get much more physical than sex. What does being in weightlessness do to an astronaut's libido? I mean, is it even possible to get a boner in zero gravity?"

"I'll be sure and bring that up at the next team meeting," Daniel said.

"A satisfied astronaut is a happy astronaut." She grinned.

"Operator ready?" rang out Margene's voice through the intercom system.

"Operator ready," someone else in the control room answered.

"Data acquisition ready?"

"Data ready."

"Light bar ready?"

"Light bar ready."

"Subject ready?"

"I'm ready," Major Purvis called out.

The centrifuge shuddered into motion.

Daniel moved to stand directly behind Taylor, leaning in close to tell her about the technical things that were going on, but she didn't hear a word he said. Her hands were quivering and she clasped them together to keep him from noticing. He wasn't even touching her, but she could feel him like a brand on her skin.

Do it. Touch him. Kiss him. Hold on to him.

Taylor clutched her hands into fists, fighting off her impulses. *No, you can't.*

She had to focus. She stared at the centrifuge as it spun poor Major Purvis faster and faster. Hypergravity. The spinning that kept you from spinning apart. Ironic.

Being near Daniel was like being in that centrifuge. All her senses tumbling, spiraling, flying out of control, while at the core, at her center, it was gravitational pull drawing her ever closer.

Magnetism. If NASA could bottle this thing between them, they could send an astronaut to Mars tomorrow.

Okay, okay. Keep cool. You can think your way through this.

She drew in a deep breath. That was the ticket. Get some oxygen to those brain cells. But it didn't help. She was doomed. A victim of her own body.

How easy it would be to turn around, frame his face in her palms and kiss him. How easy to fall blindly into chaos.

She'd fallen once and look where it had gotten her. Loving a man she shouldn't have loved. Donning every ounce of emotional armor she could muster, Taylor bit down on her lip, tossed her head, gathered her willpower and slipped weak-kneed away from him. She wasn't going to trust what felt easy when it came to Daniel.

Not ever again.

Limp with desire, she stepped away from him. But

he stuck out an arm and caught her, so now here she was lying in the crook of his arm staring up into those unforgettable blue eyes.

The kiss happened so fast it shanghaied the breath right out of her lungs. The feel of him stunned her mouth, her mind spun dizzily—like Major Purvis in that centrifuge—and her blood just *sang*.

She expected him to taste of wintergreen, as he used to. All cool and proper. But his cinnamon flavor surprised her as much as had the unexpected kiss. Hot and reckless and so not like Daniel.

Oh, this isn't good. Not good at all.

At that moment, Daniel's phone chimed, signaling he'd received a text message. His expression totally neutral, he sat her upright on her stilettos, casually straightened the lapels of his lab jacket and then turned to unclip his cell phone from his belt loop as if nothing out of the ordinary had happened—leaving Taylor staring at him, mouth agape, desperately wanting more of his kisses.

He read the text, clipped his phone back on his belt. "We've got to go," he said, his expression still frustratingly dispassionate.

Taylor wanted to scream. He'd kissed her in the observation area and he was acting as if absolutely nothing had occurred. Granted, no one in the control room could see them, and as for Major Purvis, well, he was spinning too fast to witness anything.

"Where are we going?" she snapped, irritated because he seemed so unruffled when she could hardly think.

His eyes met hers, but he showed not one ounce of emotion. "I have flight physicals to perform. The Thunderbirds are here."

WHY THE HELL did you kiss her? She's going to think it meant something. It didn't mean anything. Right? Just old times and chemistry.

Yeah right. Good thing his nurse had texted him about the test pilots. Otherwise…

Otherwise what?

I'm not thinking about that.

Taylor scurried along beside him in those mincing little high-heeled steps, her breath coming in sweet-sounding, lady-like puffs. He realized he was walking too fast for her and it was all she could do to keep from breaking into a trot.

He slowed his pace, softened his gait while at the same time another part of him was yelling, *run, run, run.*

They reached the jeep. He let her go in front of him, his gaze zeroing in on the enticing bounce of her bottom. He held the door open for her, tried his damnedest not to notice how the silky material of her pants stretched over her behind. Or how the modest V neck of her blouse looked so classy and lady-like until she leaned forward slightly and he could look straight down and see her lacy little yellow bra.

"I'm so excited," she said.

You're not the only one.

Hustling around to the drive's side, he then climbed in and started the jeep. Daniel didn't turn his head to look at her, but he knew her eyes were flashing with curiosity. Taylor was an adrenaline junkie. He thought about that time at the Governor's Mansion. How she'd lured him away from the tour and into a side room that was off limits. He should have known they'd have security cameras watching.

Come on, you did know, you just didn't care.

Yeah, well he'd been young, dumb and full of—

"Omigosh," Taylor said interrupting his thoughts as they passed the air field where the Thunderbirds' F-16s were parked.

Daniel stopped outside the medical clinic and had to admit to a bit of awe himself. The sight of those impressive fighter jets made him want to slap his palm over his heart and hum the national anthem. The slogan of Taylor's airline, Something Sexy in the Air, popped into his head. She was going to love meeting the Thunderbird pilots.

And that thought immediately brought a sour taste into his mouth.

What the hell, Corben, you jealous?

No, no, he wasn't jealous. Daniel thought as he escorted Taylor into the building. He was just—

"Doc!" The Thunderbirds' squadron leader, Lieutenant Colonel Brian "Bull" Avery greeted him with a vigorous handshake and a slap on the back. "We're here and ready for you to check the oil and kick the tires before the air show."

The Thunderbirds flew on tour from March through November. They all had complete physicals from their flight surgeon at their home base in Las Vegas before the season began, but they also received checkups before each air show. This weekend they were scheduled at Patrick.

Then Bull stepped back to admire Taylor. "Good afternoon, ma'am."

Daniel made the obligatory introductions on the way into the clinic where the remaining five members of the six-man crew were already teasing his nurse, Nathalie, as she took their vital signs.

"Holy moly," exclaimed the rascal of the group, Major Anthony "Tag" Taglioni as he jokingly snapped to attention when they entered the room. "It's Taylor Milton."

Taylor looked flattered to be recognized and why wouldn't she? Tag was a handsome bastard, high-spirited, built like a boxer and he flew fighter jets. The guy was a living breathing Top Gun.

And it was all Daniel could do to keep from wadding up his fist and punching Tag on the chin.

"You know me?" Taylor pressed her fingertips to the hollow of her throat, right above her world-class cleavage.

"Yes, ma'am," Tag said with a naughty grin. "You gave me one of the best nights of my life."

"Have we met?" Taylor asked.

"Sort of." He shrugged. "Kind of. My girlfriend and I spent a week at your fantasy resort in Japan. She took 'Make Love Like a Geisha,' I did 'Make Love Like a Samurai.' You gave a talk on tantric sex. It was awesome."

Tantric sex? Daniel rubbed his chin with his thumb and forefinger. Taylor knew tantric sex? The thought at once aroused him and made him feel inadequate.

"I'm pleased you enjoyed your stay," she said.

"You sure it wasn't the other way around," one of

Tag's team members teased. "Tag looks like he could pass for a geisha to me. What do y'all think?"

Tag shot his buddy a dirty look and hastened to add, "But that was before my girlfriend and I broke up. We're broken up now. Split the sheets a while ago."

"That's because Tag's girl wanted to be the samurai," his rowdy teammate said as an aside, winking and poking another teammate in the ribs with his elbow.

Daniel frowned. *Cocky jokesters.*

"I'm sorry to hear that about you and your girl-friend," Taylor told Tag.

"Oh, don't be, ma'am." Tag shook his head. "Easy come, easy go. It's all good."

"Let's get to the physicals," Daniel interrupted.

"Right," Tag said, hopping up on the exam table and stripping off his shirt before Daniel even told him to do so.

He noticed that Tag was eyeing Taylor to see if she noticed what he looked like with his shirt off.

Daniel also looked over at Taylor and he was surprised to find she was watching him, not Tag. He smiled and gave her a boys-will-be-boys conspiratorial expression. Taylor winked back.

In that second they were back in the observation room at the research center and he was kissing her all over again. Her mouth had been so soft and eager beneath the claim of his lips. Daniel's mind just lurched.

"So what are you doing here at Patrick?" Tag asked Taylor as Daniel put his stethoscope to Tag's back.

"Deep breath," Daniel said, "and keep quiet so I can hear."

"Yes, sir."

That stopped Tag from talking to Taylor, but it didn't stop him from looking at her. Daniel had to quell the urge to smack him upside the head.

"So, Taylor," Tag said, the minute Daniel finished listening to his breathing. "You wanna go up with the flying Thunderbirds?"

The cheeky daredevil's ace in the hole. Daniel could have smacked him.

"Really? Could I?" Taylor's eyes blazed.

Tag looked at Bull. "She's a celebrity. We can justify it."

Bull shrugged. "Sure, if she passes her physical."

Taylor looked as though someone had just granted her most heartfelt wish. Jealousy tasted like brussels sprouts—ugly and green on the back of Daniel's tongue.

"Tomorrow afternoon," Tag said. "Fifteen hundred hours. Maybe you and I could grab some dinner afterward?"

"She can't," Daniel interrupted. "Taylor has other plans for dinner."

Taylor looked surprised to learn that.

Tag looked from Daniel to Taylor and back again. Then he held up his palms in a gesture of surrender. "Hey, doc, I'm not denying I have an eye for pretty ladies, but I don't poach. If she's taken just say so."

Daniel wrapped his arm around Taylor's waist, snuggled her up tight against his hip and said, "Hands off, Taglioni. She's with me."

5

DANIEL was clearly jealous of Tag, and Taylor didn't know how to feel about that. Intrigued? Concerned? Amused? Charmed? Flattered? Optimistic? Smug? Spooked?

She decided to go with amused. It seemed the safest mood.

"So I'm with you, huh?" She flashed Daniel a smile over a late lunch at the seaside restaurant he'd taken her to after he'd finished the physicals on the crew of the Thunderbirds.

"About that—"

"No need to explain," she said, keeping her voice light and casual. She stabbed a succulent pink shrimp with a tiny fork and dipped the shrimp in cocktail sauce. "I appreciate you getting me off the hook with Tag. He's cute and all, but not my type."

"Um, yeah," Daniel said, looking surprised. "I thought he might be pestering you."

"Not a bit of jealousy going on there, huh?" She grinned. Okay, so she'd left amused and moved on to smug.

He measured off an inch with his thumb and forefinger. "Maybe just a little bit."

"Oh, you liar. You were as green as Shrek."

"You exaggerate."

"I thought you were going to punch him when he was ogling my butt."

"Don't think that it didn't cross my mind," Daniel growled.

"But I know, I know, you couldn't ruin this weekend's air show," she teased.

"Yeah, that's the reason." He locked on to her gaze. The challenging expression in his eyes erased her smug amusement and left her feeling…well…*skittish*.

An awkward silence fell between them and then Daniel cleared his throat. "So, tell me, where are you living now?"

"My father's New York penthouse. But the business keeps me busy. I'm on the road more when I'm home."

"So why are you here?"

"General Miller didn't explain that to Colonel Grayson?"

"Colonel Grayson said something about some project for a fantasy resort, but I didn't really get what he was talking about. Why don't you explain it to me?" His smile was small, but he leaned forward, showing genuine interest.

She cradled the coffee cup in her palm, absorbed the heat. "I don't think you'll approve."

"Since when did you ever care about anyone's approval?" His comment was mild, but the look in his eyes was hot.

Taylor took a deep breath. She might as well get this over with. "I revamped my father's airline."

"Of course." He nodded and leaned back in his chair. "You had to put your own personal stamp on it."

"I changed the name."

"I don't understand. Wouldn't that cause you to lose your customer base?"

"My father's customers weren't my target consumers."

"No?"

She locked eyes with him. "Have you ever heard of Eros Air and Fantasy Resorts?"

His reaction was just what she expected—startled, critical, disappointed. "I've seen the commercials. What's your provocative slogan? Something Sexy in the Air?"

"Yes," Taylor said, holding Daniel's stern, unwavering gaze. "I take full credit for the slogan and for the raging success of our airline at a time when the majority of airlines are struggling to stay out of bankruptcy. We netted two hundred and fifty million dollars in profits last year."

"Clearly sex sells," he said.

"What's wrong with that? I give people what they want, an opportunity to explore their sexual fantasies in a safe, nurturing environment."

"It's just not you. The Taylor I remembered was sexy, yes, and adventuresome in bed. But that girl would never sell out her values just to make money. What happened?"

His scoffing words knifed her. Taylor laughed, not wanting to show him how much his disapproval hurt. "You don't even know me, Daniel. We had an affair thirteen years ago for four short months when we were just dumb kids. You have no idea what my values are."

Now it was his turn to look wounded. "You're absolutely right about that. Dumb kids."

"How's your family?" she asked, changing the subject before she said something she couldn't take back. "They must be so proud of you." *I'm proud of you.*

Daniel accepted her about-face and went with it. "Mom and Dad are doing well. They live in the beach in St. Augustine. Grandpa had a stroke two years ago but he's recovered pretty well and just celebrated his eighty-fifth birthday. Jenna's married to a mechanical engineer and they live in Houston. They have a son named after me and Jenna's six months pregnant. This time they're having a little girl."

"That's really special." She meant every word she said even as a sudden wave of loneliness washed over her. "About your sister naming her son after you."

"Yeah," he said. "It's nice. I'm sorry I don't get to see them more often. I like being an uncle."

Another awkward silence descended. So much for small talk.

She dropped her gaze and busily buttered a slice of brown bread. "Um…what's going on here, Daniel?"

He reached across the table, touched her hand—touched her, hell, he *branded* her hand. "You tell me, Taylor."

She dropped the buttered bread onto her plate, sat back in her chair. Okay, no more tap-dancing around the obvious, they were getting right to it. "Apparently there's still some chemistry between us."

"Apparently."

Briefly, she closed her eyes, suppressing the shiver of arousal his voice stirred. "So what do you want to do about it?"

"What do *you* want to do about it?" he countered.

Typical Daniel. He needed a consensus in order to proceed. She wanted him to tell her that he was mad for her, that he had never stopped loving her. That he was so happy she'd walked back into his life. That—

"Because I have to tell you, Taylor, as much as I want to make love to you, I know it's not the smart thing to do." His hand was still on hers, his thumb rubbing the back of her knuckles.

"Dumb," she agreed, shaking her head while her heart cried out, *who cares what's smart, just do me, do me, do me.*

"I shouldn't have kissed you."

"Nope."

"But I did."

"Yes." Great, he'd reduced her to monosyllables.

"So I think we should just keep our distance from now on. Be strictly professional about this."

She cleared her throat. "That would be a little easier to do if you weren't holding my hand."

"Yeah," Daniel said, dropping her hand as if it was burning his. "Right."

"So no more kissing while I'm here?" she asked, trying not to sound hopeful.

"None."

"Lips to yourself."

"Hands, too," he agreed.

"Okay."

"All right."

"Great."

"Now that we have that settled…" He smiled, but it didn't reach his eyes. "Let's order key lime pie for dessert."

"BRILLIANT COVER, the girlfriend thing," Cooper Grayson told Daniel later that same day. "I should have thought of it myself."

Daniel shrugged, uncomfortable at being praised for lying to the Thunderbirds about Taylor being his girlfriend. Now it was probably all over the base. Which seemed to please his boss.

"Surprised me, though," Grayson continued. "I've never known you to be less than one-hundred-percent honest."

"It was not my most shining moment, sir."

"Still." Grayson grinned, apparently admiring his deception. "You do what you have to do for the good of the team. I respect that you can put the Air Force above your own personal values."

That made him uncomfortable, too. "I was simply trying to keep the real reason for her being here a secret, per your orders."

"Well, you did great. It's going to make things much easier when you show her around Moron. Now she'll just be there as your girlfriend. We won't have to worry about a cover story to justify her presence there. To further the illusion that you're taking a working vacation, I've booked you two in a hotel off base."

"Sir?"

"You'll be combining the conference with a romantic getaway. There's some kind of festival in Seville the same week, but I still managed to get you squared away."

Crap, this was turning into one hell of a mess. He thought about what Taylor had said to him at lunch. How straightforward she'd been about what she wanted. How he'd just stupidly ordered key lime pie instead of…instead of what? He'd been the one fool enough to kiss her in the observation room.

"Corben?"

"Yes."

"You hear me?"

"Yes, sir. You want me to take Taylor Milton to Seville as my girlfriend. Pretend we're on a romantic getaway."

"That's right. Can you handle that?"

"I will, sir." Problem was, could he uphold his promise to Taylor and keep his lips and his hands to himself in a city as mysterious and romantic as Seville?

"Keep up the good work, Corben. You're doing exactly what I need you to do."

"Thank you, sir."

"And, Daniel?"

"Yes?"

"You seem awfully tightly wound. Why don't you try to relax and have some fun?"

By FIFTEEN HUNDRED hours the following afternoon, excitement pumped through Taylor's veins, while Bull briefed her on what to expect when she flew with Tag.

"But before we can take you up, you gotta be cleared by the doc here." Bull jerked his thumb in Daniel's direction. "No one has more power over a pilot than his flight surgeon. One wrong word from him and you're grounded."

Alarm flashed through Taylor. "Daniel's going to be doing my physical exam?"

"Of course," Bull said. "He's the head honcho."

"You can't cut her any slack, doc," Tag said, "just

because she's your girlfriend. You gotta treat her as if she's one of us."

Taylor noticed Daniel ignored their teasing, but his heated gaze was clamped onto her face. Was he remembering what they'd discussed over lunch the day before? Or was he, as she was, remembering that stolen kiss?

"Are you sure you're ready for this?" he asked quietly.

Was she ready to have Daniel's hands on her, touching her bare skin in an intimate way? Not hardly.

Taylor gulped, forced a smile. If this was what it took to fly with the Thunderbirds, to research her project, then so be it. She could handle it. "Sure."

Daniel opened the exam-room door. "Go ahead and take off everything except your underwear and slip on one of those paper gowns."

Weird, hearing him telling her to get undressed in such a clinical, detached manner. It should have calmed her nerves, his professional demeanor, but instead it had the opposite effect.

He handed her an olive-green flight suit and a pair of very cool black lace-up boots. "You'll put this on after we've finished the physical, providing, of course, everything checks out."

"Okay." She took the flight suit and boots, ducked into the exam room and stripped down to her bra and panties, sorely wishing she wasn't wearing a skimpy little thong. She arranged herself on the exam table—draping the laughable paper gown that covered next to nothing over her—and rested her hands in her lap. Taylor had never felt so exposed.

It seemed to take forever but in reality it was only a couple of minutes before Daniel knocked on the door and then entered. He didn't look at her as he came into the room. He was reading the health questionnaire she'd filled out when she'd first arrived.

"I see you get regularly tested for the HIV virus," he said, his voice sounding oddly strained.

"Um…yes…a girl can never be too careful." This felt so weird.

"And you had a complete physical six months ago."

"That's right. I don't take any chances with my health. My mother died in childbirth due to complications from Type 1 diabetes."

"I remember you told me that," he said lightly.

She hazarded a glance at him, but that perfect doctor facade was firmly in place. He took his stethoscope from his lab jacket and moved toward her.

He reached for her right arm, pressed his fingertips against the pounding pulse at her wrist. He was standing so close she could feel the body heat emanating from him. "Your pulse is a little fast."

"Normally my resting pulse is around sixty. I typically run three miles a day. I'm just nervous."

"About the flight?"

"About the flight," she lied.

Taylor wasn't even thinking about the flight. Her mind couldn't process anything beyond the fact that Daniel's hands were on her and she was virtually naked. Her mind spun with a dozen fantasies. She imagined him pushing her back on the exam table and climbing right up there with her. She pictured her fingers reaching up to undo the buttons of his uniform. She visualized him tearing the skimpy panties from her hips with his bare teeth.

"Don't worry about the flight. You're in safe hands," he said. "Major Taglioni might be a hotdog, but he's top-notch and he's got the best military technology in the world to back him up."

"That's good to know."

"Most people experience some motion sickness when flying with the Thunderbirds," he said. "I'll give you a couple of air-sickness bags, just in case."

Okay, that pretty well got rid of those romantic fantasies. Thank you, Daniel.

He rubbed the bell of his stethoscope with his palm. "Warming it up," he explained. "So it won't be so cold against your back."

Then he put one hand on her shoulder and placed the stethoscope to her back above the band of her frilly pink bra. "Deep breath in."

She sucked in air like a guppy on dry land.

"Exhale."

His hand on her shoulder was so gentle and yet firm, commanding. Just like Daniel himself. A wave of sadness swept over her at all she'd lost, all she'd given away.

Inside her head she heard the words her father used to say when they watched *Casablanca* together. *When you love that deeply, you'll sacrifice for the other person's happiness. Even if it means that you have to be unhappy. That's real love. When you can let go so they can be what they need to be.*

Here's looking at you, kid, she thought.

"What's it like?" she asked, desperate to distract herself from the effects of his touch. "Riding with the Thunderbirds?"

"I don't know. I've never ridden with them." He moved the stethoscope to a new spot. "Another deep breath."

She breathed. "How come?"

"I don't meet the necessary physical requirements."

Taylor turned her head and raked her gaze over his hard-muscled body. "Huh? You look pretty fit to me." Then something horrifying occurred to her. "You're not sick, are you?"

He laughed and the warm, masculine sound lit her up inside. "No. My feet are just too big."

"Seriously? Big feet preclude you?"

"You have to be between a size five and a size twelve to fly in the F-16s. I wear a size thirteen."

"Come on, they could fudge the rules for their flight surgeon," Taylor said, incredulous. "Give you a thrill."

Daniel shook his head. "Rules are rules for a reason. I understand. And at a hundred and twelve pounds you just barely make the cut on the weight requirement. If you weighed less then a hundred and ten, you'd be grounded."

"Sounds a bit over-picky if you ask me."

"It's for your safety. You have to be strong enough to withstand the force of nine Gs. That means you'll feel the gravitational force of nine times your body weight. Negative Gs shoot blood to your brain. Positive Gs blast blood to your feet."

Taylor wondered how many Gs she was pulling now as his capable fingers explored her spine. Her head felt hot and her feet were all tingly. "Sounds scary," she admitted.

"It can be, but that's where your G-suit is going to come in. From the sheer force of gravity the suit inflates and deflates in accordance. It will squeeze you from the waist down, regulating the blood so it doesn't all go to either your head or your feet," Daniel explained.

"Sounds freaky."

"It can be unpleasant." Daniel checked her blood pressure and then put his stethoscope away. He came around to the front of the table, pulled a penlight from his pocket and checked the reaction of her pupils. "Perfect."

He checked her reflexes and then had her walk to the door so he could study her gait. She held her head high and did her best not to be embarrassed or self-conscious. This man had seen her naked and in more sexual positions than she could count. She shouldn't feel uncomfortable with him.

But that was thirteen years ago. A lifetime ago. She'd been a different person then.

And yet, on her way back to the exam table, for one fleeting second, she saw him let his professional guard down. It was there in his eyes: stark sexual desire, hungry as a wolf in winter snow.

Hungry for her.

Her gut squeezed. She flexed and tightened the muscles in her lower abdomen the way Bull had taught her in the pre-flight instruction. It was a way to combat the painful pull of nine Gs.

It worked. Instantly, the tension in her stomach eased.

"You're cleared for flight," Daniel said. "Get dressed in the flight suit and we'll fit you with the torso harness."

"Torso harness?" she echoed.

"It's what holds you in the seat."

"Sounds good," she said weakly.

She donned the flight suit and went back out into the main office where Tag, Bull, Daniel and the flight crew waited. Tag showed her how to put on the torso harness, and then Daniel helped her with the G-suit. Next came the helmet, complete with high-powered sunshades built in and the oxygen mask. Her breathing sounded raspy. She felt like Darth Vadar. "Luke." She giggled. "I'm your father."

"You can take the oxygen mask off until you're in the plane," Daniel pointed out to her and Taylor gratefully stripped it off.

"You ready?" Bull asked.

"Wait, wait," Tag said. "We almost forgot the most important part."

"What's that?" Taylor asked, feeling more than a little nervous. She couldn't believe she was about to fly with the world-famous U.S. Air Force Thunderbirds.

This was exactly the kind of opportunity she'd been hoping for when she'd asked for General Miller's help. But it wasn't just the impending flight that had her skin tingling and her blood humming. She still couldn't believe how responsive her body had been to Daniel's thoroughly professional touch.

Taylor cast a glance over at Daniel. He stood with his feet a shoulder-width apart, back to the wall, looking like the put-upon parent in a roomful of unruly kids. He caught her gaze and a faint smile picked up the corner of his mouth, as if he knew a secret and he wasn't going to share.

Bull snapped his fingers, exchanged glances with his buddy over Taylor's head "How could we have forgotten that? She can't go up without it."

"Without what?" she asked.

In unison Tag and Bull said, "A cool nickname."

"Like Tag and Bull?"

"Exactly." Tag nodded. "How 'bout TNT? You know, explosive as dynamite?"

"Too many syllables. Need something short and quick. How about Rocket?"

"Brick," Daniel said. "Her nickname is Brick."

"Like a brick house?" Tag grinned and gave the thumbs-up sign. "She *is* built for that nickname."

No, Taylor thought, her gaze locking with Daniel's. *Not like a brick house. Like a ton of bricks.*

Daniel's smile was oh-so-slight.

"Brick it is." Bull nodded.

"Come on, Brick," Tag said. "Let's go pull some Gs."

The sound of the old nickname brought back the melancholy again. She shrugged off the feeling, tilted her chin up.

The G-suit was cumbersome to walk in. She felt like the Bride of Frankenstein plodding heavily along beside Daniel, Tag and Bull as they and the support crew headed out to the airfield.

The minute Taylor spied the F-16, she fell in love. Sleek and beautiful, the jet was dressed in white with red and blue stripes. Shiny, hard, smooth. Power shimmered off her skin in waves and she smelled of liquid jet fuel.

Tag was feeling the love as well. He stood there admiring his jet, his hands cocked on his hips, stance wide. "She's the sports car of fighters. Equipped with avionics and the ability to surpass all other aircraft." He made a heartfelt sound, almost like a romantic sigh. "Our little hotties are the only ones who can pull nine Gs. F-16s are the bread and butter of the Air Force."

Taylor looked around and saw that everyone was equally moony-eyed over the impressive man-made bird.

All except for Daniel.

His eyes weren't on the jet. They were fixed on her.

Taylor's pulse jumped and she was grateful for the sunshades built into the helmet and hiding her own eyes. Unnerved, she jerked her attention back to the F-16.

Before they'd left the offices, Bull had demonstrated with a model all the maneuvers Tag would be performing that day—provided that Taylor could hold up under pressure. The drills he'd shown her all seemed impossible. How could any aircraft do stunts like that?

Once she was reclining inside, surrounded by controls and levers and blinking screens, the anxiety that had been building like the Great Wall of China against her chest slowly dissipated.

And then they were airborne, Tag doing his thing, communicating with ground control.

"Here we go," he announced to her and she got familiar real fast with the reality of pulling nine Gs.

Adrenaline shot through her system as they sailed through Cuban 8s and half loops, a maneuver where the jet stops suddenly at each point of the compass during a full-circle spin. Smooth it was not. *Nice* wasn't a word Taylor would use to describe the experience.

They flew upside down and sideways and at times, it even felt as if they'd turned inside out. Her body jerked from side to side and she was grateful for that torso harness.

And to think that during the air shows, all this was done in formation with other F-16s mere feet away.

She was impressed.

It was, quite frankly, an out-of-body experience. Taylor felt as if she were floating. She had no idea whether she was upside down, sideways or spinning in a circle. Up here, everything made sense. All directions were correct. Earth and sky were irrelevant. There was no wrong path. She had no real concept of speed. No sense of imminent danger. She was snugged serenely in her own little world.

"Yo, Brick, you with me?" Tag called out.

"Uh-huh," she said, feeling tragically sad that Daniel would never experience this.

"Don't disconnect. Try to visualize the maneuvers to keep you grounded."

Good advice. Taylor concentrated on what was happening.

Pay attention to what you're feeling. Strive to recapture it. This is what you want your clients to feel when they come to your resort.

She was in total awe. What she did not expect was the rush of emotions. Patriotism, strong and true, welled up inside her.

Daniel was part of this. These people. This team. The camaraderie of the military was undeniable and overwhelming and she finally understood why Daniel loved the Air Force. It wasn't because he condoned war or fighting. It was because in the Air Force, he truly belonged. He was a part of something bigger than himself. Something important.

A pang of envy arrowed through her, sharp and poignant. She might have this once-in-a-lifetime experience, but Daniel had had a lifetime of fitting in. Something Taylor had never had.

She wasn't the type to whine over being a poor little rich girl or cry over spilt milk. She'd been raised the way she'd been raised. Privileged, with every advantage. There was nothing to complain about. But she'd been motherless, and although her father had tried his best to make up for it, he'd been focused on his business, on leaving her a legacy.

Essentially, she'd been raised by nannies, maids and butlers. They weren't family. Not a team. Later, as her father had groomed her to take over the airline, he'd shown her how to be a leader, to be in charge, to make the tough decisions. Again, being at the top meant she wasn't part of the team. She was the boss in her ivory tower.

All alone.

Her father had taught her so much about squashing her feelings, her desires. She was adept at staying detached and letting go of love.

What he hadn't taught her—what she longed for more than anything—was knowing how to belong.

6

WHILE Taylor soared through the sky, Daniel stood rooted to the ground watching the F-16 loop and dive and twirl. He'd seen the demonstration many times, but never had his stomach paralleled each maneuver.

His gut clutched and his mouth went dry. He tried to appear completely calm in spite of the tell-tale pounding of the pulse in his throat.

Even though he knew Tag was the best of the best, he couldn't help thinking, *What if they crash? What if Taylor dies? What if I lose her again?*

You can't lose her. You don't have her. You never had her.

She was flying free as she'd always done. Leaving him behind. She'd never belonged to him. She was a conclave of one, buffered by money and her breezy self-confidence. Self-contained. Not needing anyone.

She was up there in the clouds where he could never follow, far above him, leaving Daniel feeling empty and small.

Hell, man, what's the matter with you? You've achieved your dreams. You made something of your life. You're happy for the most part. Why does it matter that she's the one thing you could never have?

Until she'd shown up on the base, he hadn't even known the old longing was still there, the sense of having missed out on something essential.

Damn him. Damn her for making him want her so badly.

Then Tag was landing the F-16 and Taylor was climbing out of the aircraft. She stripped off her oxygen mask and helmet, handing them to a member of the ground crew. Then she ran to him, cumbersome in the G-suit, eyes sparkling, hair mussed, her face rapturous with joy and passion.

"Oh, Daniel," she said sighing, looking as if she'd just had the biggest orgasm of her life. "That was magnificent."

He was so caught up in her enthusiasm, so bewitched by her verve and beauty, he took her into his arms and swung her around. She felt so perfect there.

"Look at you," he said. "Look at you."

"I didn't puke, I didn't puke," she crowed, pulling back a bit so she could look into his face. "And we pulled 9.2 Gs."

"You got yourself quite a woman there, doc." Tag slapped Daniel on the back. "She's an honorary Thunderbird for sure. I've taken up hundreds of people and they all puke. Every last one of them. But Taylor, she held it together."

A chuff of pride barreled through him, but then he had to remind himself she wasn't his woman. The honor belonged to her alone.

"It was amazing," she chattered. "Life-changing. I can't begin to describe it."

"I'm happy you had a great time." He was. That was

no lie, but he was also jealous. Tag had shown her an impressive adventure in a place where he could never go.

"Thank you," she said.

"Why thank me?" he asked. "Thank Bull and Tag."

She went up on her toes to press her lips against his ear. "You know why."

But he didn't. What was she talking about?

And then Taylor kissed him. It was quick and on the cheek, but the hell if it wasn't a kiss. And this after she had told him no more kissing.

Daniel took the hit in his groin. It was all he could do to keep from pulling her against him and kissing her properly until neither one of them could breathe.

"Aw, ain't that sweet," Tag teased. "The doc and Brick sharing a tender moment."

Taylor turned toward Tag and thanked him for the ride. Then she thanked Bull as well and shook his hand. They let her keep the Flying Thunderbirds patch they'd attached to her flight suit.

"Taylor," Tag said, "If the doc doesn't treat you right, you know where to find me."

Possessively, Daniel slung an arm around her shoulder. "Back off, Tag, I've got the power to ground you for life."

Chuckling, Tag raised his palms. "You know I'm kidding. Why don't we hit Orbit?" he said, referring to a local bar popular with the pilots. "First round is on me."

Taylor asked Daniel, "Can we?"

"You really want to go?"

"Yes, this is exactly the kind of after-hours camaraderie that would be perfect to capture for my research."

"If the doc is feeling too old and tired," Tag challenged, "you can hang with us."

Taylor's eyes sparkled and he could see she had Thunderbird fever. Daniel wasn't about to let her go alone. "I'm in," he said. "Sign me up for the second round."

That brought a cheer from the ground crew.

"Just let me go change," Taylor said and took off.

Every masculine eye on the tarmac turned to watch her walk away.

Bull leaned close. "Doc?"

"Yeah?" Daniel asked.

"If I were you, I'd get a ring on Brick's hand pronto. Half the guys here are drooling to take that woman away from you."

THEY CONVERGED on Orbit. Daniel and Taylor took their own cars. She arrived ahead of him and was already in the bar with the guys when Daniel walked in.

The place looked like something straight out of the movie *Top Gun,* complete with the ubiquitous flight groupies dangling off barstools. The only thing missing was the Righteous Brothers on the jukebox. Just as the thought popped into his head, refrains of "Unchained Melody" seeped through the speaker system.

Shit, who did that?

He looked up to see Taylor at the jukebox, her back to him, hips encased in blue jeans, swaying in time to the music. God, the woman had a spectacular ass.

She turned.

Their eyes met and for one earth-quaking moment, Daniel couldn't breathe.

What the hell was going on? Talk about sending a man mixed messages. One day she tells him to keep his hands to himself, the next day she was playing *their* song on the jukebox and looking at him like she was going to die if she didn't get next to him.

Or was she just jerking his chain the way she'd done thirteen years ago? Confused, he changed direction and headed for the bar.

Tag was there getting a pitcher of beer. "Hey, doc."

"Thanks for taking Taylor up. She really enjoyed it."

"You're welcome." Tag picked up the pitcher the bartender set down for him, but stopped, turned back. "If you're with Brick, what happened to Sandy?"

"We broke up."

"Do you mind if I give her a call?"

"She's not in a good place right now. I don't think you should toy with her."

"Who says I'd toy with her?"

"You're the biggest playboy in the sky."

"Well, maybe Sandy just needs to play a little."

"Whatever you do, don't hurt her."

"Why? Because you already hurt her enough for the both of us?"

Did Tag have feelings for his ex? Surprised, Daniel watched Tag head back to his table where a gaggle of groupies waited. Then he thought of Sandy and immediately felt guilty. Tag was right. He had hurt her enough for the both of them.

And all because he'd never really let go of Taylor.

TAYLOR WATCHED Daniel walk away and it felt as if he'd just kicked her in the gut. She'd put *their* song on the jukebox. She couldn't have been much clearer than that. And he hadn't even acknowledged her. One quick look and he'd walked away.

Maybe he doesn't even remember that it's your song.

She had to bite down hard on her bottom lip to keep it from trembling. Dammit, what was the matter with him? He's the one who'd kissed her.

Yeah, and you were the one who told him not to do it again and then you went and put "Unchained Melody" on the jukebox. You scared him off.

What in the world was she doing here? Trying to fit in where she didn't belong?

"Hey, Brick." Tag waved her over to a table where the Thunderbirds were sitting chatting up some women who looked as if they spent a lot of time hanging in Orbit. "Come on over and join us."

Not knowing what else to do, Taylor went over. Fine, if Daniel was so dense he wasn't picking up on her signals, well then she'd just sit with Tag. That ought to fry his sausages.

"Scoot over, will you, sugar?" Tag said to the blonde in the skintight micro-mini on his right. "I want my friend to sit here."

The blonde threw daggers at Taylor with her eyes, but grudgingly shifted and dragged over an empty chair from the next table.

Taylor sat beside Tag.

"You did great today," he told her.

"Thank you."

He eyed her with a glint in his eyes. "You sure you're with the doc?"

"Yes."

Tag shook his head. "That's such a shame. You and me…we could have a good time together."

"We're too much alike, Tag and you know it. We'd wear each other out in nothing flat."

"You got me there, but what a way to go." Laughing, Tag glanced away.

Taylor followed his gaze to see Daniel standing in line at the bar.

"I'm glad you guys are together. You're good for him, you know," Tag said.

"What do you mean?"

"The guy needs some shaking up and you're TNT."

"Explosives are not necessarily a good thing."

"And the way the man looks at you." Tag shook his head. "He's got passion in his eyes when he looks at you. I've never seen him look at any woman like that."

"Really?"

"He's usually all business, professional, never steps out of line, you know?"

"I know."

"You lighten him up. That's a beautiful thing."

A waitress came over to the table with a full pitcher of beer for the group.

"Here we go." Tag tipped her lavishly and she planted a kiss on his forehead. That brought a round of catcalls from the collective.

"Damn," Tag said, "I love my life." He filled his mug from the pitcher, raised it. "A toast."

"A toast," the group echoed.

"To Brick," Tag said. "A woman with a cast-iron stomach."

"To Brick," they all cheered.

For one insanely happy moment, Taylor was part of their little klatch, and then she felt Daniel's hand on her shoulder and her happiness dissolved into anxiety. She looked up to see him holding a glass of white wine.

"Brought you a chardonnay," he said, "although this being Orbit, I can't vouch for the quality."

The bubble of happiness was back, but still laced with wariness. She didn't know what to make of him.

"Thanks," she said and took the glass from him.

He stood there, looking lost and out of place.

"Have a seat, doc," Tag said, and then noticed there were no more empty seats in the vicinity.

Taylor stood up. "Would you like to play some pool?" she asked. She didn't know why she had asked that, other than she had an overwhelming need to get him away from the group. Still, she was reluctant to go somewhere more private than the bar. She didn't trust herself around him.

He surprised her by saying, "Yes."

Taylor took a sip of her wine, got up and angled toward the pool tables in the next room.

DANIEL MATCHED her stride. He still had no idea what was going on between them and he wasn't even sure he wanted it clarified, but damned if he could stay away from her. She was the sun and he was caught in her orbit.

"I should warn you," Taylor said. "My father had a billiard room while I was growing up."

"Why am I not surprised? Did he have a bowling alley, too?"

"Sadly no. I was so deprived."

"Tragic."

"It warped me for life."

"How come we never played pool in college?" he asked.

"We were too busy doing other things." She shot him a seductive look.

"I remember."

"Ah, young love."

"Correct me if I'm wrong, but I remember it more as young lust," he said.

"Same thing."

Not to me.

"You have quarters?" She held out her palm.

Daniel fumbled in his pocket, drew out the requisite amount of coins and dropped them in her hand.

She deposited them and the balls tumbled down the chute in a clatter. Taylor racked the balls, then stepped back to pick up a cue. "You break."

"Ladies first."

"Your quarters, you get dibs."

She thought she was going to beat him. He might not have played much pool in college, but he'd been stationed on several small air bases with lots of down time. He'd shot a few rounds of pool in his day.

Daniel broke. Stripes. Took his second shot, missed.

Taylor bent over the table. His gaze dropped to the curve of her luscious butt. Round and firm. He remembered exactly what it felt like to cup it in his palm.

Daniel took a sip of the long-neck beer he'd bought when he'd brought her the chardonnay. She'd balanced her wineglass on the edge of the pool table. He was getting so steamed up watching her in action, he briefly pressed the bottle to his forehead in a vain attempt to cool his rising body temperature.

She knocked in two solids, then missed and stepped back to let him have his turn.

"How come you played 'Unchained Melody'?" he asked, circling the table on her side.

"I like the song." She tucked a strand of that wickedly beautiful red hair shot through with chunky blond highlights behind one ear.

"Yeah, but there must be others on the jukebox that you like, but you picked that one. How come?" He lined up the shot, got a whiff of her ginger-scented cologne. Yesterday honeysuckle, today ginger. What a dichotomy. Sweet versus potent.

"It's a classic."

"You're toying with me, Brick." He sank the shot.

She moved out of the way so he could circle around to the other side of the table. "I'm the one doing the toying? Who's calling me by a pet nickname?"

"You used to like it."

"I used to like a lot of things."

Her comment distracted him and he flubbed the shot.

Taylor's turn at the table and she expertly sank the four ball—*whack*. Then she sauntered toward him, her gaze locked on his. He couldn't think of anything at that moment except how gorgeous she looked with those brown eyes shimmering like fondue chocolate.

She wrapped her adroit fingers around the cue and slowly slid the shaft back and forth. Her bottom lip tucked up between her teeth, her eyes on the ball as she concentrated.

His imagination went wild.

Stop it. Stop ogling her, stop thinking about sleeping with her. You've got to break the news to her that she's going to Spain with you, like it or not.

Crap, he'd forgotten about that.

Bam! She sank the third shot.

"What are your plans for this weekend?" he asked.

She raised her head. "Are you asking me out?"

"No," he said, "I'm asking you to Spain."

"Wow, aren't you moving a little fast? I mean we haven't even had a first date." She scratched.

Daniel took his turn. "We had our first date thirteen years ago."

"Still," she said. "A trip overseas seems a bit presumptuous."

"But you're not against it?"

"What's in it for me?"

That rattled him. "You get to see a TAL sight."

"Excuse me?"

He explained what a TAL site was.

"So this proposition is strictly business?"

"Yes."

"Let me get this straight, rather than be here during the shuttle launch next week you want me to go to Spain with you and hang around some moldy little air base on the very off-off-off chance that the space shuttle might have to abort there? And I don't get any nookie out of the deal, either?"

She shocked him, but he wasn't about to let her know it. Daniel smiled. "Something along those lines."

"Why would I do that?"

"Killer tapas?"

She shook her head.

"There's a flamenco festival in Seville at the same time." His ball did not go in the pocket and she took over again.

"Keep talking."

He was out of ideas. "The pleasure of my company."

"Non-sexual company?"

"That's right."

Taylor glanced up from where she was bent over the table. "Care to make it interesting?"

Her words—and her position with her butt in the air—sent his libido into the red zone. It had been a long time since he'd been this aroused. "Huh?"

"You win, I go to Spain with you."

His mouth was so dry with anticipation he had to lick his lips before replying. "And if you win?"

"Sex and lots of it."

She kept moving around the table, making one difficult shot after another, cleaning his plow, as his granddad would have said. Finally, there were just three balls left. Two of his stripes and the eight ball.

"Eight ball in the center pocket," she called out and then executed it like a pro.

She'd won.

Applause broke out.

That's when Daniel realized the Thunderbirds, their flight crew and various and sundry girlfriends, groupies and wives were standing in the doorway razzing him.

"Way to go, Brick."

"She kicked your ass, doc."

"Better stock up on condoms."

Startled Daniel ran a hand over his head, his grin embarrassed.

Taylor held out her hand. "Pay up."

"Huh?" What was she expecting? Sex, right now? Tonight? He wasn't mentally prepared for this no matter how badly he wanted her physically.

"You heard me." She stood gazing at him, heat simmering in brown eyes deep as the Grand Canyon.

The group hooted at Daniel and he smiled, chagrinned.

"YOU'RE NOT going to hold me to a pool-table promise," he said as they picked up their drinks and moved over to let Tag and the blonde in the micro-mini take over their table.

"What? Are you reneging on your word?" Taylor teased.

"You were really serious?"

Daniel looked so panic-stricken, that she almost let him off the hook, but then she recalled what Tag had said and decided that Daniel needed a little shaking up in his life. He'd grown stodgy in his accomplishments. It wouldn't hurt to string him along a bit. "All I know is that you made an agreement and now you're backing out."

"I want to renegotiate the terms."

"Too late," she said. "I've already won."

She didn't know why she was doing this. Why she'd even made the wager in the first place. Why she was holding him to it. A smart woman would ask Colonel Grayson for a different escort. Let Daniel go on to Spain and she could just stay right here and watch the launch from Cape Canaveral exactly as she'd planned to do when she'd first conceived of this research project.

What, and miss out on all the sex?

You can't force the guy to have sex with you.

"I have to go to Spain, Taylor," he said. "And I really hope you'll come with me."

"And the sex...?" Why was she pushing this? Why couldn't she just let well enough alone? Going up in that fighter jet today had only underscored what she already knew. A relationship with Daniel was bound to have no future.

She was all about the fantasy. It was why she'd decided to add the resorts to the airline's repertoire. Reality sucked. Fantasy on the other hand was a sweet escape.

And she loved the whole *Top Gun* thing going on here tonight. It was exactly the kind of fantasy she wanted to capture so that her guests could experience it, too.

"And the sex?" she repeated, amazed at her own persistence. When he didn't answer, she held her breath, wondering if he was just going to keep ignoring what she'd asked. Then Daniel said the magic words that convinced her to go to Spain.

"I'm not ruling out the possibility."

7

I‌t w‌a‌s Taylor's second trip to Seville.

Her first foray had been while researching the myth of Don Juan for her Legendary European Lovers itinerary four years earlier and she'd quickly become enamored with the country. The Andalusian culture was filled with mystery, pathos, seduction and romance. She had promised herself that one day she'd come back here. She'd just never expected to return on an Air Force transport jet with Daniel Corben, of all people, as her escort.

The plane ride over had been uneventful. Surrounded by Air Force personnel, she and Daniel had had no privacy. Which was all right with Taylor. Much safer to spend the time on her laptop catching up on work and making plans for the new resort than to share sultry glances with the man who made her throb in a hundred different ways. Especially since they hadn't resolved the sex-versus-no-sex issue.

But uneventful didn't mean her body wasn't taut with sexual tension. Every time Daniel looked her way her pulse revved like an F-16 engine. Running high and hot. And if the way he gripped the armrest every time their legs accidentally brushed was any indication, he was feeling just as raw and achy as she was.

They landed at Moron Air Force Base. Daniel had arranged to borrow a military vehicle to use while they were driving back and forth from the city to the air base.

"Why aren't we staying at Moron?" she'd asked.

"For your comfort," Daniel said. "Military housing can be a bit stark and accommodations are limited at a base this small, particularly with military personnel converging for the launch day disaster drill."

"I'm not a princess. I won't whine if there's a pea under my mattress. I can stay on base."

"Trust me. You're accustomed to the Four Seasons, it's better this way. Don't worry. I'll be staying in town with you."

She couldn't help feeling a bit patronized and wondered why he was really stashing her away in the city. In the end, she'd given up trying to persuade him to let her stay on base. She did want to see the sights and attend *La Feria de Sevilla,* the city's annual spring festival.

The subtropical weather of Seville in late April was warm and inviting and the city buzzed with fiesta activities. Tourists and locals alike clogged the streets, many dressed in vibrant costumes, the men in the bolero hats and the short cropped jackets associated with Andalusia, the women in sexy, flamboyant flamenco dresses, large shawls, intricate earrings and colorful hair combs.

Seville itself was architectural poetry, a mosaic daydream. A succulent fantasy of tile and sunshine. A blending of cultures—Moorish, Arabian, Roman, Flemish—created a unique and compelling style.

When Taylor had come here alone four years ago in the wake of her father's death, she'd imagined traversing these streets with someone special. A lover, fiancé, husband.

She had pictured herself and this anonymous lover walking hand in hand through the narrow winding *Calle de las Sierpes* on the north side of the spacious palm-shaded *Plaza Nueva*. Imagined them taking flamenco lessons together. Rowing a boat along the Guadalquivir River. Eating tapas and drinking sherry at Calle Betis in Triana until the wee hours of the morning in accordance with the laid-back, late-night Spanish tradition.

And wickedly stealing a kiss inside the sacred Cathedral of Seville.

Taylor's body flushed at the thought of it. Here she was with the one man in the world she most wanted to be with and yet, it was not on the right terms, not in the right context. He wasn't her lover. Not anymore.

But he could be again.

She wasn't deceiving herself. The chemistry was still there—hotter than ever in fact. Sizzling and surging between them. It wouldn't take much to seduce him. She could feel it.

To what end? Nothing had changed. They were still night and day. Different in every way possible.

To what end? Dumb question. How about hot sex? What could be more simple than that?

It sounded simple, but Taylor wasn't that stupid. One night with Daniel wouldn't be enough. She'd want more and wanting more…well…*that* path was loaded with nothing but pain. Been there, walked it, got the awful bruises to prove it.

When they arrived at the hotel, Daniel took command,

pushing his way through the throng of tourists crowding the lobby, speaking flawless Spanish to the desk clerk.

Taylor was agog. "When did you learn Spanish?" she asked while they waited for the clerk to look up their reservation.

"When I was stationed at Moron right after I finished my residency."

It made her feel faint to think he could have been here at the same time she'd been here. "So this is a homecoming for you."

"It's one of the reasons I was asked to head the medical team in the disaster drill. That and the research I'm involved in on the physiological effects of extended weightlessness."

And is it the real reason you don't want me staying at the air base? That thought stung. Was he ashamed of her?

"You're a man of mystery, Daniel Corben."

"Not so much. You're the mystery, Taylor."

She cocked her head to study him. She couldn't tell if he was tense or if it was simply his crisp military posture that kept him so distant. "How so?"

"Señor Corben, here is the key to your room," the desk clerk interrupted, passing him a key card. "You are on the top floor overlooking the gardens. It's one of our best rooms."

"Thank you. Now let's get Ms. Milton squared away."

"Pardon?"

"We'll need a room for Ms. Milton."

The clerk looked from Daniel to Taylor and back again. "The *señora* is sharing your room, no?"

"No," Taylor and Daniel said in unison.

A worried frown puckered the clerk's brow. "I am

afraid some mistake has been made. The reservations clearly state you are booked for one room only."

"Grayson," Daniel muttered.

"Excuse me?" Taylor inclined her head.

"This is Colonel Grayson's doing." He shook his head and said to the desk clerk, "We need a second room."

The man held up his hands. "That is completely impossible, Señor Corben. We are booked solid for the entire week of the festival and so is every room in Seville."

Daniel blew out his breath and ran a palm down the back of his head. Taylor recognized the gesture. He was stressed.

"Maybe we should just go back to Moron," she suggested.

"I'm sure they're full up with people flying in for the disaster drill. No point driving all the way back there only to find there's nowhere else to stay." He inclined his head.

"I don't mind sharing a room if you don't," she said, feeling as if she'd just stuck her head in the open mouth of a wild lion.

"She is a beautiful woman," the desk clerk said, trying to be helpful. "Sharing a room should not be such a hard thing to do."

"Harder than you ever imagined," Daniel muttered.

Taylor caught the sexual innuendo in his words and snickered. "How hard?" she whispered.

"We're talking mahogany, sweetheart."

"Right now?"

He shrugged, looked sheepish. "I'm just saying

it's a damn good thing that I'm holding a suitcase in front of me."

"Daniel!"

"You look shocked." His eyes met hers. "Why do you look so shocked, Taylor? You were never easily shocked before and I never made a secret over how you affected me."

"Still? I can still cause you to…um…" She glanced down.

"So it seems."

Did he regret the fact that she could still make him hard in the middle of a crowded hotel lobby without even touching him? Come to think of it, how did she feel about that bit of earth-shaking news?

"Mahogany?" The desk clerk frowned in confusion. "I do not understand this American term."

"It's okay, Javier." Daniel read the man's nametag. "Believe me, I don't understand it, either."

Javier raised a hopeful eyebrow. "So you take the room? It is good?"

Daniel's eyes met Taylor's eyes again. "It is good?"

"It is good," she confirmed, even though her pulse fluttered in her throat like kites in a hurricane.

He laughed and his face was transformed from ruggedly attractive to heart-stoppingly handsome. Laugh lines crinkled around his eyes and sent her stomach free-falling.

Javier started laughing, too. Taylor found it infectious and joined in.

"You go now." Javier waved them aside and focused on the next person in line.

"Looks like we've been dismissed."

"Looks like."

They stood there, each waiting for the other to make the first move.

"After you," he said, keeping their suitcases clutched tightly in his hands.

She couldn't help herself. Her gaze strayed.

"Hey," he said, maneuvering the suitcase around to block her perusal. "The elevators are that way." He nodded to his right.

Taylor covered her mouth with her hand to hide her grin. She didn't want him thinking she was laughing at him.

"I'm sorry about this," he apologized, once they were in the elevator. They kept their eyes trained on the numbers over the doors.

The elevator stopped on the top floor and they stepped off. Daniel consulted the room number written on the paper sleeve the key card came in. "Room 787. Looks like we're at the very end of the corridor."

"You sure you don't want me to carry my own suitcase?"

"I've got it."

"We can do this, you know," Taylor encouraged, her voice coming out high and reedy. "Share a room."

Daniel nodded. "Absolutely."

"We're adults, we can control ourselves."

"Totally."

"Nothing's going to happen," she added as he ran the key card through the card reader.

"Not a thing."

"Celibacy is a grand thing."

"Completely underrated," he agreed, pushing open

the door and stepping aside to let her walk over the threshold.

The minute they were both inside they turned to stare at each other.

Instantly, Daniel dropped the bags and Taylor jumped into his arms.

He made a deep sound of masculine arousal, threaded one hand through her hair at the nape of her neck and gently, but firmly pulled her head back, then he took her mouth with his.

His lips were hard, but sweet, oh so sweet. Honey and maple syrup mixed together. She sighed, half surrender, half pleasure, and just drank him in.

His erection pressed hard through the material of his uniform pants. Joy strummed through her as Daniel's tongue pushed past her parted lips and she felt the power of him drill straight into her bones. Her ears sang a hallelujah chorus. Her nose twitched with the salty smell of his skin. She closed her eyes to deepen the cinnamon taste of him.

It was as if an invisible vice had been fitted around her body and was slowly squeezing out all the air. Emotions burst inside her—desire and attraction, longing and craving, trepidation, excitement, nervous energy and most damnable of all—hope.

What are you doing? Nothing has changed. Daniel is still Doctor Military—dedicated and dutiful and you're still...well...you.

She'd broken up with him thirteen years ago for a very good reason. The reason was still valid.

This doesn't have to be happily-ever-after. It could just be happily-ever-orgasm. Great sex with an old friend.

Because she knew it would be great. Sex had always been great with Daniel. Hell, better than great. His love-making had been world-class.

But could she have sex with him and then just walk away? How did she protect her heart? Breaking up with him the first time had almost killed her soul. Did she possess the right stuff to walk away a second time?

She couldn't think straight. His kiss was a searing brand, claiming her as his own.

His lips made her quiver.

She mewled a soft sound of pleasure. He wrapped his arms around her waist and drew her up tight against the expanse of his chest.

Taylor was surprised by his strength, but she shouldn't have been. She already knew he was a steady, sturdy man. Built for endurance. Strong and centered.

Honorable. Dutiful. Idealistic. Committed.

Her total opposite.

She was fast-paced and quick-witted. Built for flash and show. Strong, yes, but obsessed with work, focused always on the goal, unable to stop and smell the flowers. Where he was honorable, she was a business-woman. Where he was dutiful, she was a rebel. Where he was idealistic, she was cynical.

His tongue explored her mouth as if he was deter-mined to unearth every secret she'd ever kept.

Taylor melted.

"Aw," he murmured against her lips. "You taste like sunshine, Brick."

Her pulse swirled.

This second kiss was fiercer than the first—more de-manding, urgent, skipping beyond subtleties to unveil the hungry animal lurking inside the controlled man. A beast yanking at its chain. This kiss told her Daniel Corben was not as restrained as he seemed.

The idea frightened her.

But thrilled her even more.

The commanding pressure of his lips induced a response so intense it felt as if time and space vanished and she was left toeing a tightrope across a bottomless abyss.

He sucked the breath right out of her body, leaving her weak-kneed and giddy. Her mind spun a dozen ridiculous what-if fantasies.

Daniel kissed her harder and deeper, holding on to her as if he couldn't get enough. He made her feel powerful and cherished and terrified.

Taylor teetered.

Caught on the twin horns of desire and common sense, she registered that this was crazy, this longing for something she'd lost years ago. It was something they could never get back. Too much time had passed, too much water under the bridge.

But while her mind was chattering, Daniel was doing unbelievable things to her. Slick heat gushed through her body. The muscles deep within her pelvis tightened. Her heart raced and she surprised herself by how quickly she grew wet for him.

Lust consumed her. She had to have him. Had to have him or she would surely die. She ran her tongue around his lips and he made a masculine noise of enjoyment.

And that's when things got very interesting.

He cupped her face in his palms, dipped his head and kissed her again with a soul-stealing, grade-A, world-class kiss that curled Taylor's toes.

The moment was brilliant. Life was brilliant. He was brilliant.

The next thing she knew they were tearing off each other's clothes. Thirteen years fell away and they were those horny college kids again, madly passionate about each other.

Yes, yes.

Her fingers grappled with the buttons of his shirt at the same time she was tossing off her shoes. The sounds he made were pure encouragement.

He grabbed the hem of her blouse and stripped it over her head. They punctuated the undressing with more desperate kisses.

More, more.

She could kiss him a thousand times and it would never be enough.

DANIEL WAS swept away. The rational part of his brain seemed to have short-circuited. Common sense? Out the window. Prudence? What was that? Logic? Who could be logical when Taylor's mouth tasted so delicious, when the flat of her belly felt so soft beneath his palms? When her scent turned his dick to granite?

He was nothing but a core of hard, throbbing need and she was the cause of it all.

His arms were around her waist and they were spinning for the bed, her skirt and his pants getting shucked off along the way. They stumbled, but managed to hold on to each other and somehow made it to the mattress without falling down.

"Daniel, Daniel." She sighed.

"Taylor."

They were both breathing hard and she sat straddling his bare abdomen. Her gorgeous breasts were still harnessed in a purple bra with a front clasp. He reached up and set the beauties free. They burst forth in creamy abundance. He couldn't wait to taste them.

Her eyes lit up and she gave him the full force of her smile. Looking at her like this was like leafing through a treasured memory book. A photo album filled with things you never wanted to forget.

Oh, but she was beautiful.

Suddenly, he felt shaky inside, like a rattletrap building that had been condemned.

His gaze met hers and instantly he was hung in the past, remembering the first time they'd made love in his off-campus bachelor apartment. He wanted her just as much now as he'd wanted her then.

Maybe even more so.

He could scarcely believe she was here with him, that he was getting a second chance with her. A second chance at love.

Whoa, slow down. No one said anything about love.

Thirteen years ago she'd made it perfectly clear she was in it only for the sex. Why would things be any different now?

Don't jump the gun. Don't throw your heart into this so quickly. That's where you made your mistake before. You rushed her.

She touched him. Boldly, right between the legs, reaching around to cup his balls in her palm. Mind-blowing pleasure rocked him and Daniel hissed in air through clenched teeth.

"You like that?" she cooed and seductively lowered her long, thick lashes.

"You know I do," he growled. "You know too damned much about me."

"Not any more than you know about me."

"Do you still like to have your fingers sucked?" he asked, then took hold of her wrists and slowly drew her pinkie finger into his mouth.

She tossed her head, wriggled against him.

He chuckled. "I'll take that as a yes."

She leaned forward to kiss him, her body tight against the length of his, her soft breasts pressed against his hard chest, her lovely little rump resting on his pubic bone just above his jutting cock.

Daniel kissed her, hugged her, rocked her.

She laughed and the sound was sweeter than music. It was the thing he'd missed most about Taylor, her free-spirited laughter. He couldn't hold out a second longer. He had to have her and he had to have her now.

"You got a condom?" she whispered hoarsely. "Because I can't take this waiting. I need you inside me now."

Daniel groaned.

"What?"

He slapped a palm to his forehead. "No condoms."

She made a sound of exasperation. "You're a doctor. How can you not have condoms?"

"You run a resort specializing in sexual fantasies, how can *you* not have condoms?"

"I didn't want to presume anything." She laughed and pressed the tip of her tongue to her upper lip and he just about came undone. He was about to say, "to hell with condoms" and make love to her anyway. "What's your excuse?" she asked.

"I purposely didn't bring any exactly for this reason," he replied. "I wanted to make sure that if I was too weak-willed to control myself, not having any condoms would make me stop and think before crossing the line."

"You seriously thought about having sex with me?"

"Taylor, I haven't thought about anything else since you drove onto my Air Force base." He paused. "You doubt this?" He took her hand and guided it to his throbbing cock.

"I think it's a good thing," she said, breathing as if she'd just sprinted across a football field. "That you left the condoms at home. You were right. Gives us time to think things through before we do something stupid."

"Not me. I think it's the second-dumbest thing I ever did."

"What was the first dumbest?"

"Letting you break up with me."

She looked away, and then slid off the bed. He was terrified he'd said absolutely the wrong thing at absolutely the wrong time. She picked her purple silk panties off the floor and wriggled into them. He couldn't help watching her breasts jiggle.

"Taylor?" he ventured, sitting up. "You okay?"

She faced him, a strained smile on her lips. She zipped up her skirt, grabbed her bra off the bed. Was there anything she couldn't shrug off? He both envied and distrusted her ability to so quickly and easily shove

her emotions aside, change negative feelings with a determined shrug to the contrary.

"I'm fine as long as we get out of here. Otherwise,
I can't be held accountable for my actions."

8

THEY SPENT THE REMAINDER of the day sightseeing, but Taylor seemed very subdued, not at all her normal high-spirited self. They talked about the space shuttle program and her research and his job as a flight surgeon, but they avoided talking about anything too intimate.

They strolled through the beautiful example of Moorish Revival in Spanish architecture, *Plaza de España*. The plaza was built in 1929 to host the Spanish-American exposition and it was used as a backdrop in the Star Wars movies. The Plaza was a huge half circle ringed with buildings that housed, for the most part, government offices. Numerous bridges made the Plaza accessible over the moat and in the center sat a large fountain.

A group of tourists were tossing coins in the fountain. Daniel noticed a tall gangly man in a Hawaiian-print shirt with a camera slung around his neck staring at Taylor.

No surprise there, the woman was a stunner. Daniel felt at once both proud and ready to punch the guy's lights out when he raised the camera and snapped a photo of Taylor.

"You have an admirer," he said.

"What?"

"Bean pole in the luau shirt just took your picture."

"Where?"

Daniel looked back but the guy had already disappeared in the crowd. "Guess he took off."

Taylor frowned. "What did he look like?

Daniel described him. "Do you know the guy?"

She shook her head. "I don't think so, and it's probably nothing, but there's been some trouble at my resort in Venice."

"What kind of trouble?"

She told him about the smoke detectors and the fire, about the guests getting food poisoning and the stolen Renoir. And about the undercover reporter.

"You think it could be the same guy?"

"Probably not. It's probably nothing. I get a little paranoid sometimes. There's a lot of competition in the airline business."

"You think the guy could be a corporate spy?"

Taylor shrugged. "It wouldn't be the first time I've had people follow me. But honestly, the only people who know I'm in Spain with you are my executive assistant and Colonel Grayson, and I know you guys want to keep my presence here as quiet as I do."

"I never considered everything you must deal with in the course of your job."

Taylor gave a humorless laugh. "You have no idea. I get threats on pretty much a weekly basis."

"Serious ones?"

She waved a dismissive hand. "Ninety-nine percent of them are crackpots."

Daniel flexed his fists. "And the one percent who aren't?"

"They're the ones who make me paranoid."

"You should hire a bodyguard."

"You know me. I hate to have my movements restricted."

Yeah, he knew. Daniel drew in a deep breath. He knew he had no right to tell her how to live her life, but it didn't stop him from worrying about her.

"Hey," Taylor said in a lighter tone. "Let's rent a rowboat and cruise the moat."

"All right." Daniel nodded, realizing she didn't want to talk about it any more, and he reached out to take her hand.

It quickened his heart when she squeezed his palm and gave him a soft smile.

They rented a boat and joined the flotilla of little crafts bobbing around the moat. Daniel rowed for a while, and then stopped underneath a quiet bridge just as the sun was drifting down the horizon and the lights in the Plaza flickered on. It was a romantic spot in a romantic city with a romantic woman.

She lapsed into silence, staring out at the water.

"What's on your mind?" he prodded. "You still thinking about that camera-happy tourist?"

"No." She shook her head. "I was thinking about the first time I came to Seville. It was right after my dad died."

"Business trip?"

"No, actually. Seville is where he and my mother went on their honeymoon. I guess you could say the visit was a pilgrimage." Her words were tinged with sadness. "I was trying to make sense of it. Trying to say goodbye."

"You came alone?"

"I did." She trailed her fingers in the water. "But I always hoped to come back some day in happier circumstances." She fell silent.

Daniel let her be for a few minutes and then he said, "Are you all right?"

"I'm fine, doc."

"This is it then."

She met his eyes. "What?"

"The real Taylor."

Her eyes widened.

"The quiet, serious Taylor behind all the spontaneous, free-spirited, soar-like-an-eagle stuff. The Taylor you don't want anyone to see."

"Your medical degree is in psychiatry, is it?"

"I've never seen this side of you."

"That's because it's depressing."

"There's nothing wrong with being sad."

She inhaled audibly. "When you love someone you always lose them."

"Death is a part of life."

"A part I don't like."

"No one does."

"So what's the point of loving?"

"To be alive now. To grasp what's in front of you and live life to the fullest."

"Exactly. That's exactly what I try to do. With my resorts, with my life. I want to give people an oasis from pain."

"Pain is inescapable." Daniel recognized what a huge moment this was for her, even if she didn't. She was opening up, talking to him, really talking to him. He realized how often in the past she'd used sex and fun as a cover-up, a way to avoid dealing with weighty issues like death and loss and pain.

"You don't have to tell me that."

Daniel held her gaze. "What do you want?"

"I want it back."

"What?"

"My childhood, my mother, my father, you…"

The last word that fell from her lips snatched all the air from his lungs.

"But that's not going to happen, is it? No. The best I can hope for is closure. Right? That's why I came to Seville before and it looks like it's why I'm here now."

Daniel shifted in the boat and it bobbed on the water. "I wish I could help."

"You want to help me forget?"

"I do."

"Then kiss me. Kiss me so hard I can't even think. Kiss me until pleasure is all I feel."

"Taylor," he murmured, pulling her into his arms and kissing her, even though he knew the price of this pleasure would eventually have to be pain.

He wondered what would have happened if he hadn't joined the Air Force, hadn't followed in the footsteps of tradition like his father and grandfather. He might be a different man today. More sophisticated, more open-minded, more accomplished in love relationships. But he *had* joined the military and he *had* become a doctor and his love life had been severely neglected because of his choices.

And he was suffering for it now.

To fight his feelings of inadequacy, he did the only thing he knew how to do well. He took control, startling Taylor with the demanding pressure of his lips.

He could tell she was thinking, *I can't let him get away with this.*

She tried at that point to take over, folding her slender arms around his neck and pulling him down into the bottom of the boat. Fighting to maintain a position of dominance was in her nature. He had already figured that out about her, noted the same instinct within himself. In that respect they were two of a kind, although in almost every other way they were exact opposites.

She was playful and coy and impulsive. He was taciturn and serious and precise. She was wind-blown. He was spit and polish. She lived to surprise. He embarrassed easily. She danced to the beat of a different drummer. He marched to the tune of the "Battle Hymn of the Republic." She was a Lamborghini and he was a Chevy sedan.

And he loved her just as much now as he had thirteen years ago. Maybe even more.

She kissed him, increasing the passion, upping the tempo. Her lips blasted him into another realm of awareness, making him concentrate on the feel of her mouth under his. Her manicured fingernails dug into the back of his head. A deep-pink flush of arousal painted her face, spread down her neck. She was ready for action. She left no doubts about it.

The flick of her tongue over his teeth was lazy, sultry, teasing him by degrees. Slowly at first, but then with steadily building pressure.

Her body was so perfect: her waist so narrow that his hands spread could almost span her. And his fingers were itching to do just that and so much more. Aching to skim every part of her, to learn all the secrets her body possessed.

But this wasn't the place to sate his desires. He

pulled back, stopping just at the point of no return, separating his mouth from hers.

"Hey," he said shakily. "Let's save that for later. Right now, I'm starving. How about you?"

She sat up, straightened her blouse, ran a hand through her hair. "Yeah, okay, all right."

But it didn't feel all right.

He smiled, trying to pretend everything was just peachy. He reached for the oars, started to row. They passed under the next bridge, brightly lit against the night. He looked up and that's when he saw him.

It was the tall man in the Hawaiian shirt, camera in hand, leaning over the railing and staring down at Taylor with a malicious gleam in his eyes.

AFTER THEY left the *Plaza de España*, Taylor and Daniel got caught up in the festival crowd flowing through the streets. Even at eight o'clock in the evening, heat rippled in the air while the sun hunkered on the western sky, awash in purple and orange.

Ground zero for *Feria de Abril* was a mile-long temporary city of tents, called *casetas*, erected on *Real de la Feria* near the Guadalquivir River, which wasn't far from their hotel. The *casetas*—set up as makeshift dance halls—were made of brightly striped canvas and decorated with thousands of multicolored paper lanterns. Aristocratic Spanish families, trade unions, clubs and political parties hosted the *casetas* and each had its own unique vibe and personality. Some were exclusive to members and invited guests only, but others were open to all, with commercial bars tucked inside.

The foot traffic surged across the intersection.

Daniel took Taylor's hand so they wouldn't get separated, but once the throng thinned out, he enjoyed holding her hand so much, he didn't let go. Nor did she pull away.

Latent breezes stirred smells and sounds on the night air. The uniquely Andalusian scent of slate and granite-scented soil melded with the sounds of whinnying horses. The spicy tang of cumin, rosemary, sage and grilled chorizo spoke of laughter and dancing. The earthy aroma of table grapes accented the soul-stirring lament of Spanish guitars.

"I know the perfect place for tapas," Daniel told Taylor, "if it's still there."

"Sounds yummy." She rubbed her stomach. "Let's go."

He took her to *El Rincocillo,* one of the oldest and most popular tapas bars in Seville, favored by locals and tourists alike. It was still early for the supper hour so they were able to get a table after only a short wait. They ordered a variety of tapas and a carafe of sherry.

The restaurant was alive with layered flavors—caramelized onions, roasted garlic, briny olives, musty white truffles, the gentle undertones of saffron. Daniel's mouth watered instantly, but not because of the food. What triggered his taste buds was the way Taylor looped her arm through his and leaned into him, giving him a heady whiff of her own fragrance—clove, rose, black spruce mingling in a tangy grapefruit oil base.

She was the only woman he'd ever known who changed her perfume with her moods. Most women settled on an aroma they liked and used it for a lifetime. But not Taylor. By sheer volume of variety, she made herself a standout.

"Oh my God, these tapas are to die for. It's like eating starbursts of delight. Seriously, you've gotta try a bite." She scooped up a big forkful of the tasty tidbits called *Queso Frito AlinAdo con Salsa de Escalona*, which translated into fried cheese with shallot sauce.

Cupping her palm underneath the fork, Taylor leaned across the table to hold the offering up to his lips.

"I have my own fork," he said.

"What? You afraid of eating after me? I don't have cooties, I promise. Get my shots regularly and everything."

"It's not that."

"What is it?"

"You're dripping cheese."

"So what?"

He glanced around the restaurant feeling as if everyone was watching them. No one was.

"Come on." She waggled the fork. "I know you want a taste."

"Just eat it, Taylor."

"I know what it is. You're afraid of looking undignified. Aw, that's so cute. If your hair was long enough, I'd muss it just to loosen you up."

"You're loose enough for the both of us. I think it's time to lay off the sherry."

"Ouch." She grinned and rubbed her shoulders. "Want your blade back, Brutus?"

Damn, but he couldn't help grinning in return. He chuckled, shook his head. He'd missed her fun-loving wit.

"That's it. That's the way I like to see you. Now taste the fried cheese." She poised the fork before him again.

"It's artery-stopping."

"Only if you indulge all the time. Everything in moderation, right, doc?"

He might as well eat the damn thing. Clearly, she wasn't going to stop badgering him until he did. Daniel dipped his head, opened his mouth and Taylor slipped the tines of her fork between his teeth.

"Hey," he said as the creamy blend of flavors melted on his tongue. "That *is* delicious."

"Told you." She licked cheese off her fingers.

The woman was so unconventional. Not a behavior you'd expect from an airline heiress. But he shouldn't have been surprised. Taylor was the most sensual person he'd ever known.

"You've forgotten how to have fun," she said.

"I don't know that I ever did."

"You did when we were together."

"Only because of you. I tried things I never would have tried just to impress you and then I pretended I did them all the time."

"Like what?"

"Hot-air ballooning, wine-tasting, water-skiing."

"You didn't fool me with the water-skiing," she said. "I pretty much figured out you were a virgin when it took you two hours to get up on the skis."

"But you never said anything, why not?"

"What? And blow your macho image?" She took a bite of the second tapas dish, spicy little meatballs called *Albondigas*.

"Can I have some of that?"

"Oh, now you come crawling."

"What can I say? You've convinced me to take a walk on the wild side."

"Only if you let me feed it to you and stop looking around to see if anyone is watching. No one cares if we're canoodling with food."

She was right. But he'd spent a lifetime toeing the line, doing the right thing, following the rules so closely that even something as simple as allowing her to feed him felt hedonistic.

"Live a little," Taylor whispered, slipping a morsel of *Albondigas* between his parted lips. "Let yourself go for once, doc. You don't have to always be healing or protecting someone. There *is* life beyond aerospace medicine."

Taste was such an intimate sense. You couldn't take it at a distance. You had to be up close and personal to dig in. The way Taylor ate—with gusto and reverence—was as individual as her fingerprints. He thought of Sandy, who never ate with her fingers. She always cut her food into tiny little morsels and watched her caloric intake as though it was a religion. Neat, tidy, conscientious, the kind of traits he'd told himself he should want in a woman, but didn't.

He wanted a bold, messy, passionate woman who grabbed life by the throat and didn't let go. A woman who could fly in an F-16 and not get sick. A woman who could shoot pool like a hustler. A woman who gave one hundred and ten percent.

He wanted Taylor.

Daniel had forgotten exactly how good being with her made him feel. Whenever he was around her he felt lighter, freer, more relaxed. Taylor was a tropical vacation. Breezy, easy, warm and smooth.

"Do you remember when we went to Padre Island on spring break?" she asked.

"When the unseasonable hurricane blew in? How could I forget?" He smiled.

"And I wanted to go parasurfing and you wouldn't let me and I accused you of being a stodgy old codger?"

"You would have killed yourself."

"I know." She grinned. "Thanks for saving my butt."

She reached out a hand to stroke his upper thigh. Her touch was so unexpected, so elemental, Daniel grabbed his glass of sherry and downed a big swallow.

"Do you remember?" she asked, her voice low and husky, "what we did while we waited out the storm?"

"We battened down the hatches…"

"And?" She leaned in closer.

"Made good use of our alone time."

She walked her fingers along his neck, whispered in his ear, "And?"

"Woman," he growled. "You keep this up and we'll be buying the biggest box of condoms in Seville to take back to the hotel room with us."

9

AFTER DINNER, they strolled hand in hand through the *Real de la Feria* looking for appealing public *casetas* to visit. The eager crowd jostled them along. They passed vendors hawking all things flamenco—costumes, jewelry, combs, shawls, castanets.

Taylor stopped to admire the array of colorful dresses, her mind warmly fuzzy with sherry, her stomach stuffed with tapas. A flamboyant red-and-black polka-dot flamenco dress caught her eye.

"You'd look gorgeous in that," Daniel said. "Then again, you look gorgeous in anything. Or in nothing."

She turned her head and grinned at him. His eyes shone with a lustful light.

"Get it," he said.

"Only if you'll get a matador costume." She shifted to the men's side of the tent and fingered the gold brocade on the bullfighter's jacket.

"Oh, no." He held up both palms.

"Why not?" Taylor teased him. "We could get you a bolero hat and whip and we could go back to the room and play Indiana Jones meets a gypsy princess."

"Olé," he croaked.

"Is there a place we can try this on?" she asked the squat, dark-haired woman behind the counter.

The woman pointed silently to a curtained-off section at the back of the tent.

"Here," Taylor directed, pulling the matador jacket off the hanger and thrusting it in Daniel's hand. Try this on." She scouted out a pair of tight black matador pants. "These, too."

To her surprise, he took the garments and disappeared behind the curtain.

"Don't forget this," she called to him, tossing a bolero hat over the top of the curtain of the makeshift dressing-room stall.

Taylor browsed while she waited, picking out a black shawl and some matching combs to go with the ruffled flamenco dress.

"You dance flamenco?" asked the clerk in hesitant English.

"No." Taylor shook her head.

"With him." The woman nodded toward the curtain. "You should dance."

Taylor grinned. "I'm working on that."

"My sister…she teach."

"Your sister teaches the flamenco?"

"Yes." The woman bobbed her head again. "When you dance flamenco for a man, you make love to him."

"Very poetic."

The woman reached behind the counter and pulled out a flyer advertising the flamenco dancing services of one Señora Delgado, complete with a hand-drawn map to her nearby *caseta*. "Go. See my sister. She teach you."

Just then, the curtain was drawn back and Daniel emerged in the matador costume. Both Taylor and the shop vendor drew in audible gulps of air at the sight of him.

At once, he looked like artist and athlete, as if he could indeed be a true torero, stylish and brave. The pants molded to his muscular thighs, clung to his lean hips. The jacket accentuated his broad, straight shoulders. The hat, rakishly tipped slightly to one side, heightened the arrogant appeal of his sheer masculinity. Talk about your tall, dark and handsome.

Taylor's knees wobbled and her mouth went dry. "Olé." She breathed.

"I feel like an idiot," he said.

"No, no," Taylor and the costume vendor exclaimed in unison.

"You look great," Taylor assured him.

"Perfect," the woman added.

Another female customer shopping the narrow aisle stopped, stepped back and offered a thumbs-up along with a lingering look that ran from Daniel's head all the way down the length of his body. Then she said something in Spanish that was clearly flirtatious.

"You look too good," Taylor said. "Maybe you shouldn't get it."

Daniel grinned and winked at her. "You started this. I'm getting this and you're getting the flamenco dress. You got me all revved up about the gypsy-princess fantasy."

"Sometimes I'm my own worst enemy," Taylor muttered.

"Go put on your dress," he said. "If I'm wearing this, you're going to match."

She had to admit the fantasy set her heart thumping and her mind whirling with potential scenarios. When she emerged, he stared at her as appreciatively as she'd stared at him.

They stowed their regular clothing in the shopping bag the happy vendor provided and walked out into the street readily blending in with the rest of the costumed crowd. Walking beside her handsome torero, who kept drawing admiring glances from surrounding females, Taylor forgot about Señora Delgado's flamenco dance school until they passed her *caseta* with a large hand-painted sign in both Spanish and English posted outside the tent.

Learn the seductive dance of flamenco now. Make love like an Andalusian tonight.

Clearly, the pitch was aimed at tourists. Taylor knew the flamenco was a complicated discipline—just as complex as ballet or jazz—that took years of practice to master, but still, a dance lesson was bound to be fun and something she might consider incorporating into the Legendary European Lovers resort itinerary.

She tugged Daniel toward Señora Delgado's dance studio.

"Whoa," he said pulling back. "I did the costume, you want me to take dance lessons, too?"

"One lesson." She shrugged, grinned impishly.

"Taylor…"

"Please, Daniel," she cajoled.

"I think you like making me look ridiculous."

"I like showing you how to laugh at life. At yourself."

"I'm probably gonna regret this, but lead on," Daniel acquiesced.

The minute Señora Delgado saw them, her eyes lit up. The tent was empty except for three guitarists, placidly plucking out a forlorn folk tune. She greeted them in Spanish and Daniel responded in kind, and that widened her toothy smile.

She held out her palm. He passed her the required amount of money for the lesson.

Señora Delgado began with some history of the flamenco, which Daniel translated for Taylor's benefit. "She says that nomadic gypsies from North India brought their dance traditions to Andalusia. Southern Spain at the time was a real melting pot of Roman, Moorish, Jewish and Indian people. The roots grow from the peasant class, but the music, the dance, it touches the heart and soul of everyone who comes into contact with it. It possesses universal appeal."

"She's milking the romance, huh?" Taylor said.

"For sure." Daniel winked.

"Flamenco," Señora Delgado continued in Spanish as Daniel translated. "Is a balance, a blend of passion and control."

The guitarist changed rhythm with the dance instructor's storytelling.

"Like American Jazz," Daniel continued the translation. "Flamenco is improvisation. The dancer is overcome by spontaneous response to the spirit, but the movements are all about pattern and structure. You cannot have one without the other. It's like man and woman in balance. *Duende.*"

"What does that mean?" Taylor asked Daniel. *"Duende?"*

"Literally translated," he said. "It means *goblin* or *fairy,* but to the flamenco dancer it signifies the inner emotional force that fuels the performance."

"You don't see good flamenco," Señora Delgado

said in English. "You feel it in your soul." Expressively, she thumped her chest, just over her heart, with a fist.

"Dramatic," Taylor observed.

"Ultimately, flamenco is about connection."

The guitar music quickened. Señora Delgado raised her long, lithe arms over her head and began her seductive, serpentine movements. Suddenly, from the back of the room, a costumed man appeared. His booted feet tapping rapidly, rhythmically, he danced toward her like a rooster courting his hen.

A dozen people came through the back entrance of the *caseta*—all costumed Andalusians: men, women, children. They were clapping and snapping their fingers in time to the music and shouting, "Olé" or *"Baile! Baile!"*

The entire *caseta* burned with life and color and romance. From the folds of her dress, Señora Delgado produced an intricately designed fan. She snapped it seductively at the male dancer, then turned and murmured something to Daniel.

"What did she say?" Taylor whispered, overwhelmed with the pageantry.

"She wants me to imitate him and for you to imitate her movements."

"Baile! Baile!" cried the spectators.

Señora Delgado made exaggerated hand gestures and waited for Taylor to mimic her.

Taylor followed as best she could, raising her arms above her head, moving them like a rose opening to the sun. With her hips, she swished the skirt of her dress, stomped her feet along with the plucking guitar strings and snapping fingers.

While Taylor followed Señora Delgado, Daniel was doing an amazing job of keeping up with the Spanish woman's partner. His shoulders were back, his posture open, he rotated his wrist, seducing Taylor with his come-hither movements.

On and on they danced, each step taking them deeper into the mysterious dream of flamenco. At some point they stopped watching their teachers and let the music overtake them.

Daniel and Taylor had eyes for only each other.

They were connected. With the music, with the dance, with each other. Physically and emotionally, their bodies communicated in ways mere speech could not.

They weren't even remotely performing the correct footwork, but it didn't matter. No technique at all, but the emotion. It was raw and primal and real. The *Duende* swept them up in an orgy of the senses.

Perspiration flowed from their brows. The tent smelled of midnight—sultry and dark. Everyone in the room was dancing now, a jumble of writhing arms and tapping legs.

The music reached a crescendo.

Taylor looked into Daniel's face, saw the flame of desire burning in his eyes and she was lost, just *lost*.

Then everything went silent.

"Lesson over," Señora Delgado concluded as her troops filed from the back of the tent.

Taylor and Daniel exchanged glances and burst out laughing. He took her hand and they strolled breathlessly from the *caseta*.

"Wow, that was…" Speechless, she couldn't think of a word to describe the experience.

"Intense?" Daniel supplied. "Yeah, it was."

"I've never felt anything quite like it."

"It was fun. I'm glad you talked me into it."

"You're welcome."

"And I've never seen you looking more beautiful than you look tonight," he told her.

"More beautiful than when I was twenty?"

"Far more beautiful," he confirmed. "You have a grace and wisdom about you that you didn't have then."

Throughout the tent city of *Real de la Feria* the sound of dueling flamenco guitars rose up, fierce as a great African lion calling his pride. They stood listening to the mesmerizing sound of the deeply soulful melodies. Taylor felt the resonance echo within her. Standing here, watching Daniel silhouetted in lamplight from the multitude of colorful lanterns, she experienced true flamenco.

He tugged her to one side of the *casetas,* in a dark, secret corner, out of the way of foot traffic, deep into the night. The danger seeped under her skin, burrowed into her veins, quickened her heart. Suddenly, she was afraid but she had no idea why.

Daniel placed both hands on her shoulders and softly whispered, "Taylor, Taylor."

She felt his lips on the back of her neck, and then his teeth slowly nibbled up one side. She heard the crisp rustle of her flamenco dress as his hand reached up to cup her breast, his thumb idly brushing her nipple.

He pressed her closer to him. She heard the sound of his breathing strong and steady. His teeth captured her earlobe and he gently chewed the tender flesh.

She moaned and arched against his mouth.

Thoroughly, ravenously, he kissed her and she kissed him back with the same starving wildness.

Her body was on fire for him. Blood pulsed through her, hot and frustrated. She moved her head closer, grazing her lips against his. He showered her with rich, tender kisses.

His erection was rock-hard and she yearned for him to plunge deep inside her. Daniel's thick masculine scent filled her nostrils as he cradled her against him. He ran one hand down her bare arm, tickling gently.

"I've got to have you," Daniel gasped. "Let's go back to the hotel. Now."

"Condoms first," she panted, her lips throbbing from the pressure of his mouth. "You get them while I hit the ladies' room."

"Yes, ma'am." Daniel saluted her. "Meet you back here in ten minutes."

Daniel disappeared in the direction of the shops lining the street opposite the entrance to the tent city, while Taylor wound her way through the *casetas* trying to remember when she'd seen the sign for the ladies' room.

It was only after Daniel had disappeared from sight that Taylor realized she was alone in a foreign city, foggy-headed with desire and drunk on flamenco.

The lanterns threw dark shadows into the corners. Corners where anyone with ulterior motives could lurk. The skin on the back of her neck prickled and goose-bumps spread over her forearms.

That's when Taylor knew she was being watched.

The impulse to run nearly overcame her. But her limbs were locked, she couldn't move.

Don't freak out. Of course you're being watched. You're a woman alone in the midst of a bacchanal.

Slowly, she scanned the darkness. She spied a dozen

masculine faces peering at her from the passing crowd. Self-consciously, she tightened her shawl around her shoulders, the ladies' room forgotten.

She was an interloper, an outsider. This was not her element. Then again, she should be used to feeling that way by now. She'd never truly fit in anywhere.

One particularly ugly man leered at her, stuck out his tongue, waggled it in a lewd gesture. Disgusted, she turned down the narrow walkway between two *casetas*.

A shadow fell across her.

She looked up, gasped.

A tall, ominous figure in a long, black hooded monk's robe towered over her, wearing the most sinister mask she'd ever seen. It was a skeleton face with distorted features. In his hand he carried a bullfighter's lance. She knew death when she saw it.

The figure laughed, deep and wicked.

She froze, trapped in the surreal moment, praying this was all some disturbing nightmare.

Without a word, he simply shouldered his lance and walked around her.

Taylor blew out a shaky breath. She was on edge. Between the vandalisms at her resorts and the sexual tension between her and Daniel, Taylor's nerves were frayed to the breaking point.

Then from out of the darkness, a forceful arm snaked around her waist.

Taylor let out a weighted scream and brought her arm down, already into the martial arts moves she'd learned when researching her Japanese resort.

Her elbow connected with a muscular abdomen.

"Ooph."

She heard her attacker's exhalation of breath, and if her foot hadn't gotten tangled in the ruffled skirt of the damned flamenco dress, she would have kicked him to his knees. She stumbled, staggered, whirled around.

Masculine hands encircled her wrists. "Stop, Taylor, it's me. It's Daniel."

She looked up into those familiar blue eyes and all her fears vanished. He held out his arms. She sank into his embrace, buried her nose against his jacket.

"Hey, hey," he murmured, gently stroking her cheek with the back of his hand. "You're trembling."

"I got scared," she confessed, trying hard not to start crying with relief. "The crowd. The darkness. My foolish imagination got the better of me."

"My fault," he said, nuzzling the crown of her head with his chin. "Totally my fault."

"It was nothing. I was jumping at shadows."

"I shouldn't have left you alone. I don't know what the hell I was thinking. Who am I kidding? I wasn't thinking. I was operating on pure testosterone." His voice was low and rumbly, his tension evident in his wordiness.

"It's okay," she reassured, stepping back, putting some distance between them to staunch the vulnerable sensation. She shouldn't rely on him. It was a bad idea to let him comfort her. Having sex with him was one thing, depending on him was another thing entirely and she wasn't about to let herself get caught up in needing him.

"You don't look okay." He took her chin in his palm, tilted her face up to meet his gaze.

She shook off her fear, forced a smile. "I'm just a little overstimulated, that's all."

He ran a hand down her arm, his face pinched with concern. "You sure you're all right?"

A lump formed in her throat, but she swallowed past it, keeping things light. "Right as rain, just as long as you got those condoms."

10

BY THE TIME they got back to the hotel room, things had calmed down and Daniel was second-guessing what had seemed so urgent back at the *Real de la Feria*.

Sex.

His dick was still hard and the condoms were in his pocket and he wanted Taylor with a force that damn near blinded him in its intensity, but on the walk over, his logical, rational, Dudley Do-Right side had kicked in, and it was whipping his ass.

Because no matter how hard he tried, Daniel couldn't make it all about sex. Not with Taylor. Whenever he held her, he felt like a kid again and it was Christmas morning and he'd gotten everything he'd asked Santa for.

And that worried him—a lot more than he wanted to admit. Taylor had broken his heart once, did he really want to go back for seconds?

You're different now. You're tougher. Stronger. Wiser.

Taylor was different, too. Less frivolous, more focused. She was a businesswoman and had a down-to-earth aura about her that shored up the girlish spontaneity. Her father's death and her subsequent inheritance of his airline had probably instigated those changes in her.

But she still had that restless edginess that made her jump at shadows and fight imaginary attackers. She was used to taking care of herself, depending on no one, and for some unfathomable reason the thought made him profoundly sad.

Daniel didn't know what he would do if he didn't have his family, his friends and the Air Force to rely on. He couldn't imagine such a lonely, isolated life.

"Hey there, big guy," Taylor said, drawing his attention back to the moment. Back to her.

"Hey there."

"You still with me? You had a faraway look in your eyes."

"Right here, Brick."

Dammit, he shouldn't have called her by that nickname. Not when he was feeling so conflicted.

The seductive smile Taylor shot him sent old Dudley Do-Right scrambling to pack his bags. *Screw doing the right thing. Screw getting hurt.* He had to have this woman or die.

Daniel wrapped his arms around Taylor, pulled her up tight against his chest and kissed her as if the world was going to end tomorrow.

She twisted away, broke the kiss. "Daniel…"

"Yeah?" he asked, his brain slick with hormones. "What is it, babe? Tell me what you need and I'll deliver."

Taylor splayed a palm against his chest, pushed back a little. "Just to be clear, this isn't about anything more than a hook-up. No expectations. Right? No promises."

"No reunited lovers," he said, ignoring the squeeze of his gut.

"That's right." Her smiled seemed falsely bright.

"No strings attached. Gotcha."

"Can you handle it?"

"The most I'm hoping for besides a helluva good time in the sack is a little closure."

"Closure," she echoed.

"I never felt like we ended things right. This gives us the opportunity for one last hurrah." *And a chance for me finally to stop comparing every woman I meet to you.*

"Yes." She nodded. "That's it. Maybe even give you a chance for a little revenge. I know I hurt you and I'm sorry for it."

"Not as much as you've probably imagined," he lied. "I recovered pretty quick."

"Oh," she said. "Well, that's good to hear."

Daniel had to be honest with himself even if he wasn't being honest with her. That damned Dudley Do-Right syndrome again. He had, in fact, fantasized about using sex to get even with her for leading him on and then dumping him. The motive had been born of pain and inexperienced youth and he wasn't proud of the impulse, but yeah, he'd pictured himself screwing her within an inch of her life, then walking away, leaving her begging for more, begging for him.

But he no longer had such an impulse. All he wanted now was to be with her. Even if only for a little while. Life was short and they were together right now. Daniel would take what he could get and be grateful for it.

No matter the emotional cost.

"Why sexual-fantasy resorts?" he asked her as they entered the elevator that would take them up to their room.

"Pardon?"

"Why did you add sexual-fantasy resorts to your father's airline?" The elevator opened and they got off on their floor.

"I needed something edgy, something different."

"So you put your personal touch on air travel."

She smiled. "I did."

"Do you enjoy making other people's sexual fantasies come true?" He slid the key card through the reader, opened the door.

Her face lit up. "I truly do. When I get letters from couples telling me how a week at my resort saved their marriage—well, it makes me feel good."

"So how about you?"

"What about me?"

"What's *your* favorite romantic fantasy?" Daniel asked, flicking on the bathroom light as they walked in, but leaving the light in the main room off.

"Huh?" Taylor blinked, caught off guard by the question.

"This is all about pleasure, right? Having a good time, enjoying ourselves." He reached out to toy with an errant strand of hair that had fallen from the comb.

"Um…I don't know."

"Come on. You create fantasy resorts for a living. Are you seriously telling me that you don't have a favorite romantic fantasy of your own?"

"With so many to choose from, who could play favorites? But right now, I am liking Indiana Jones and the gypsy princess."

"That's a possibility," he conceded. "But I'm dressed as a bullfighter."

"True."

"I'm determined to get to the bottom of your deepest sexual fantasy."

"Oh-ho?"

"Oh, yes."

"How's that?"

"What's your favorite romantic movie?"

"Casablanca," she said without thinking twice.

"So…your favorite fantasy is to be abandoned by your lover for the sake of honor and duty? Interesting psychology, Ms. Milton."

That jolted her, so she laughed. "Don't read so much into my movie selection, Dr. Corben."

"Okay, what's your second-favorite movie?"

"Shakespeare in Love."

"I'm beginning to see a pattern here. Unlucky in love—"

"Lucky in career."

His gaze softened. "I remember your favorite book."

She swallowed. "What's that?"

"Tale of Two Cities. You were rereading it for the fifth time when we met. Remember what you told me?"

"No," she whispered.

"You said there was nothing more romantic than sacrificing your life for another's. I wonder if that's what appealed to you about me. I was joining the Air Force and you were hung up on the romantic idea of a man who would sacrifice everything—even his own life—for the woman he loved."

"It's just a book."

He nailed her with his gaze. "You're used to being sad, aren't you? I never realized that about you before.

How sad you are underneath the money and the glamour and the fantasy lifestyle."

"Who, me?" She shook her head, simultaneously shrugged, but she could barely pull in air, he was so damned on target. "No, of course not. You know me. Free-wheeling. Fun-loving. Go, go, go."

"Denying your pain won't take it away."

"Not denying. Nothing to deny. Pain-free. That's me."

"I want to be honest here."

"Okay."

"How about this then?" He kissed her, hotter and more explosive than before.

"Ah," she panted when he paused several minutes later. "Now that's what I'm talking about. Pure sex."

The heated look in his ice-blue eyes was worshipful. He sank onto the mattress, staring at her as if she was stark-naked.

Taylor immediately felt self-conscious in the red-and-black polka-dotted flamenco costume that draped all the way down to her ankles. How could she feel so exposed in a dress that covered so much of her body?

"Take off your clothes," he commanded, stretching out his long frame and propping himself up on his forearms so he could watch her. The balance of power shifted. He was in control and she could do nothing except follow orders.

She swallowed, pulse jack-hammering in her throat and started for the buttons on her dress.

"No, your hair first. Take it down. Nice and slow."

Lowering her eyes, she cocked her head and, with measured movements, dragged the comb from her hair.

After that, she raked her fingers through her hair, tousled it, shook it down the back of her shoulders.

"Now the dress." His voice was like a knife in the dark of the room. Sharp and pointed.

Taylor continued their fluid dance of seduction, taking her time with the buttons, stopping once in awhile to throw him suggestive looks, moaning softly when her own hand grazed her breasts. When she finished opening all the buttons, she stood there looking at him, making sure that the slant of light from the bathroom illuminated her from behind, displaying her silhouette.

He sucked in an audible breath.

Taylor smiled smugly.

"Keep going."

She shimmied the dress down to her waist, past her hips and then let it pool on the floor at her feet in a flouncy, red-and-black polka-dotted ripple.

"Now the panties." His husky voice razed her control. He was undressing, too. Wrestling from the matador costume, kicking off his boots, getting naked on the bed. He stripped off his underwear and his penis jutted forth, a glorious flesh-colored pole. She couldn't wait to slide down it.

Excitement trembled her hands.

"Go slow." He palmed his penis, moved his hand up and down in time to her swaying rhythm.

She inched down the tiny pink silk panties, sending gooseflesh popping up all over her tingling skin. The lower she went the faster her pulse pounded. Finally, they were down around her ankles.

"Toss your panties to me."

She lifted her leg and with a deft flick of her foot sent the panties flying toward the bed.

Daniel grabbed them with one hand and grinning, brought them to his nose. "Ah," he said, "smells like your sex."

Her cheeks flamed hot.

He fisted her panties and lay back on the pillows, a shaded, predatory expression on his face. "Off with the bra."

She prolonged the process, unsnapping her bra hook by hook with excruciating leisure, heightening the eroticism, growing wetter the longer the undressing took. Coyly, she inched the strap down her right arm and then her left. By the strap, she twirled the garment around the index finger of her left hand and let it go. The bra landed on Daniel's grinning face.

Bull's-eye.

She giggled. His laughter filled the room.

"Come here." He patted the mattress beside him.

Taylor went.

He surprised her with his tenderness. He'd been talking so tough she thought he was going to take her hard and rough. She'd braced herself for it, prepared to surrender to him in a carnal, heated rush. Her mind was so set on that scenario that when he lightly skimmed his fingertips over her bare skin, she came unwound completely.

Daniel was a glory to look at. Toned and hard and leanly muscled. His pecs flexed and rippled when he moved and Taylor admitted she was having trouble breathing. The hotel room was suddenly stifling in spite of the air conditioning.

His breathing was heavy, a rough, sexy noise that caused her nipples to bead up tight. His skin was damp with perspiration, as was hers. The scent of his pheromones enticed her. She craved the smell of him.

Taylor licked her lips.

He banded one arm around her waist and pulled her down atop him. He snuggled her against the rigid length of him and tugged her down to fit his hot mouth over her aching nipple and his deep groan of appreciation matched her own.

Her hips twitched against his pelvis, the muscles between her thighs clenched hungrily. He reached for her breasts with his hands but she grabbed him by the wrists and pinned them above his head.

"No hands," she commanded.

He made a guttural sound of despair. "What do you have up your sleeve?"

"Wouldn't you like to know?

His penis jerked hard against her inner thigh. With one hand still pinning his wrists in place over his head, she ducked her head and gently nipped one of his nipples through the thin material of his muscle shirt.

He gasped and writhed and swore.

She licked her way up his body, his chin and his jaw, stopping just long enough to work over his earlobe. When she raised her head, she discovered he was staring at her with a gaze so blazingly lusty she felt as if she'd been singed.

The pulse in his wrist leapt hard and fast and she knew he was just as turned-on as she. Taylor loved how quickly she was loosening him up, how swiftly he was reading her. Just like old times.

Now all she had to do was push him over the edge, make him totally lose control.

Taylor slid back down the length of him, her tongue savoring the salty taste of his hot skin—tasting, licking, exploring. He moaned when her lips closed over his shaft.

He became harder, close to bursting as she licked him, and she reveled in her femininity. She loved him with her mouth, caressed him with her tongue, coaxing him to the edge of ecstasy. His body was stone.

"Don't make me come," he whispered. "Not yet. I want to be inside you." He lifted her up, kissed her tenderly as if she was the most treasured thing on earth.

She moaned, loving and yet hating, the sweet torture. She wriggled against his hardness, her breasts pressed flush against his chest.

He flipped her over, his turn to be in the driver's seat and ran his fingertips up and down her shoulders. She threw back her head and he trailed his kisses to the underside of her neck, nuzzling and nibbling. He rubbed his thumbs over her nipples and they beaded so tight that they hurt.

"Ah," he said. "So you still like that?"

"It's awesome."

A languid heat draped over her, thick with sexual urgency. She wanted him so badly. Her need was a solid, unyielding mass in her throat.

"What about this?" He laved his tongue along the underside of her jaw.

She shuddered against him.

"And this?" Lightly, he tickled the skin on the inside of her upper arm.

"Wicked." She gasped.

"Precisely." He grinned.

When his mouth found its way back to hers, Taylor heard nothing except for the drumming of her heartbeat, tasted nothing except for the searing flavor of his erotic tongue.

The force of his kiss made her tremble and sweat. Her knees quivered. Her heart pounded.

He tunneled his fingers through her hair. She felt his presence in every cell of her body, in every breath she took, in every strum of the blood pumping through her veins.

He loved her with his mouth, the way she'd loved him, tonguing her with amazing tenderness, a slow glide from the sensitive spot behind her knee, around to her kneecap and up her inner thigh until she was rolling in ecstasy.

She floated, detached. She was total awareness, her entire body throbbing with sexual energy.

He kissed languid circles of heat and she was transfixed. Finally he edged to the spot where she wanted him to be, at the sweet V between her legs.

When his full wet lips locked on to her, she imagined she was a succulent summer peach, ripe for the taking. His wet tongue teased, slowly licking her outer lips. He buried his face in her. Inhaled her. And then he caressed her with the sensuous sweep of his tongue.

He sucked at every fold, lapped at her ridges. She lifted her buttocks to deliver his meal. An electric flash of brilliant energy lit the inside of her head and all the air was drained from her lungs.

She surfed his tongue, owned it. She hovered on the brink of orgasm but he would not let her fall over. A steady humming vibration began deep in her throat, emerging as a wild moan. She thrust herself against his mouth, gripped the sides of his head with her thighs, letting her juices flow.

He released his hold but wouldn't remove his tongue from her twitching clit. His tongue danced with it, wriggling nimbly around and around until she moved from easy cha-cha to frenetic flamenco.

Her skin was incredibly sensitive, her body tingling and tender. She tried to push him away, it was simply too much pleasure, but he stayed put, pushing his tongue deeper inside. Then out again and down to the region beyond.

This new sensation drove her into a frenzy.

Her muscles flexed. Her world quaked.

His fingers touched and tickled. Her butt, her inner thigh, her clit. He slid one finger deep inside her wetness, while his tongue continued to strum the feminine head of her.

She didn't know where she was or who she was with. Who was she? Woman or creature?

Madly, frantically, they grappled with each other. His hands were strong and warm. His mouth an instrument of exquisite torture. Time spun, morphed, as elusive as aerospace.

She was embraced by a longing so sweet and severe she couldn't breathe.

In delicious anguish, she cried out her delight.

Daniel rocked back on his heels, clasped her to his chest and held her tight until her crazy thudding heart calmed.

Then, when she had rested, he made love to her again, sinking his flesh into hers. He was her lover and he wanted her desperately and she wanted him right back with the same high-octane intensity.

The entire time he was buried inside her he stared deeply into her eyes, as if he was lost in her gaze and could not find his way out. Did not even want to find his way out.

They were one.

Mated.

Trembling and clinging to each other.

His cock filled her up, pushing deep inside her until he could go no further.

Then he pulled back.

In and out, he moved in a smooth rhythm that rocked her soul. He rode her and she rode him until they both came in a searing, white, blinding light.

DANIEL and Taylor sat up in bed, spent and exhausted. The ceiling fan overhead circled lazily, stirring the sheet lightly covering their sweat-dampened bodies.

"Whew," Taylor said, blowing the hair from her eyes with a puff of breath.

"How was it for you?" he asked.

"I just said *whew.*"

"It could mean whew, you're glad it's over."

"Nervous about your performance?" She tickled his ribs.

"Hell, yes," he admitted. She looked so damned good lying there next to him. Being with her again felt like old times. Scratch that, it was better than old times. "It's been thirteen years."

"And like fine wine, you've ripened with age, my

sweet." Her smile put his gut into a tailspin. "Now, you get to return the compliment. How was I?"

"There are no words," he answered honestly.

"That bad, huh?"

Instead of answering, he leaned over and planted a raspberry on her bare belly, causing her to collapse in a gale of laughter. When he was with her he felt twenty-two again.

She threaded her fingers through his hair, pulled his head back so she could kiss him. He twisted around in bed and hauled her up against his chest, her warm, sexy scent filling his nostrils. "Dammit, Taylor but I'm having a good time."

"Me, too. We should have done this closure thing a long time ago." She nibbled his chin.

Daniel groaned. "You love torturing me."

"I didn't hear any complaints." She was watching him through heavy-lidded eyes, her pleasure obvious.

"You're so beautiful," he said.

She ducked her head, traced a fingertip along his chest. "You're not half bad yourself."

He ran his hands through her hair. "I like those golden streaks you added to your red hair."

"Ah-ha, I knew it. You're secretly a fan of blondes."

"I'm a fan of whatever hair color you're sporting."

"You are a silver-tongued devil."

They looked into each other's eyes and Daniel felt the earth shift. He wanted to tell her he'd missed her. That he was happy to have her back in his life again, but he was too afraid of ruining things to voice that thought. Hell, he was too afraid to even have that thought.

"So what made you decide to make aerospace the

theme of your new resort?" he asked so he wouldn't say what he was thinking. "It's not the kind of slam-dunk erotic premise people would expect."

"I disagree. Space travel is very sexy."

"Only to people who don't work in it."

"I suppose it was a natural extension of revamping the airline. The new frontier so to speak."

"I have a feeling you're going to be first in line to offer your customers space travel when it becomes as common as air travel."

"I doubt I'll be around to see that."

He shook his head. "Don't be so sure. Technology is on the verge of bringing mind-boggling changes to the space program."

"Do tell."

"In the not too distant future, people will be able to take vacations in outer space."

"Hang on," Taylor said, crawling out of bed and padding over to her purse. "I need to take notes."

Daniel watched her sashay back to the bed, pen and notepad in hand. With each sway of her hips, his heart bumped.

She curled back up beside him. "Okay, let's brainstorm."

"Brainstorm?"

"I need your expertise in designing my resort."

"I'm a doctor, not a NASA engineer."

"My customers don't want the nitty-gritty details. They just want a romantic facsimile. This is about indulging their sexual fantasies, not actually flying to the space station."

"Okay, okay," he capitulated, laughing.

They spent the next hour brainstorming ideas for Taylor's aerospace-themed resort. Daniel was surprised to discover how much he enjoyed helping her come up with ideas. It was creative and fun. He couldn't help but think how little fun he'd had in his adult life and how much he liked being with her again. This sudden longing for all that he'd missed out on took him by surprise.

By nature he was a methodical ordered guy. He preferred to know all the rules before tackling tasks. He had rigid views on life and he prided himself on doing the right thing, even when doing the wrong thing was the most difficult choice. But part of him wished he could relax a little. Let himself off the hook. Stop being such a reasonable man.

"This is brilliant," Taylor said some time after three o'clock in the morning.

Daniel couldn't believe it was that late. He hadn't stayed up that late since...had he ever stayed up that late?

In college, when you were dating Taylor.

Taylor made him want to stay up twenty-four hours around the clock so he wouldn't miss a minute with her.

"You're brilliant."

She kissed the end of his nose and giggled. Her light, carefree sound touched something in him. "Flatterer. You're just trying to make up for not telling me how great I am in bed."

The memory of what they'd just shared was burned into his brain. He wanted more.

He wanted her.

Closure. This was about closure. Shutting the door on the past. One last goodbye. That's all it was. He shouldn't expect anything more. It was just as stupid to expect anything more from her now as it had been thirteen years ago. Taylor was who she was. A free spirit. And he was who he was—rooted, traditional, a conformist.

"What's got you furrowing that handsome brow?" she asked, running her fingertips along his forehead.

"Huh?"

"You've got that intense look that says you're thinking too hard. Stop thinking so hard, Daniel, this isn't rocket science. Or tell me what you're concentrating on so hard so I can help you think." She screwed up her own features in a thoughtful expression, clearly poking gentle fun at him.

"You really want to know what I'm thinking about?"

Her eyes widened and she nodded.

"This," he said, taking her hand in his and guiding it to his erection and said, "This is what's on my mind."

11

THEY NEVER slept. When the alarm clock went off at six, they were in the middle of their third session of exquisite lovemaking.

"You stop what you're doing to slap that alarm clock and I'm slapping you," Taylor hissed, riding the wave, heading straight for her fifth explosive orgasm of the night.

"Now that's something we haven't tried."

"Not into pain, babe. I know you've figured that out about me by now," she teased.

Daniel chuckled, but he never broke stride. Within seconds he was coming inside her again.

At one point during the night Taylor had told him, "You have to get some sleep. You're helming the medical team for tomorrow's disaster drill."

"I've got the rest of my life to sleep," he'd replied. "I've only got you for a few more days. If for nothing else, medical school, internships and residency teach you how to function without much sleep. I can handle it. Now come here."

And so she'd surrendered to the all night sex-a-thon. It hadn't been a tough sell. But now, in the jeep headed over to Moron, she kept yawning behind her palm.

Snap to attention. You've got a big day ahead.

Daniel, however, seemed no worse for wear. If anything, the man looked rejuvenated. His eyes glowed and his cheeks possessed a high color and he had an extra spring in his step.

They entered the base and he took her to meet the commander, Colonel Linda Bennett. Apparently they were old friends because Linda greeted Daniel with a fierce hug. "Danny Boy, it's been ages since we've seen you. You're looking fit."

"Thanks." Daniel beamed, put his arm around Taylor's waist and drew her closer to him. "I want you to meet—"

"You must be Sandy!" Linda interrupted and clasped Taylor's hand. "Daniel's told me so much about you. Welcome to Moron. We're so happy to have you with us. We might be small here, but you'll soon see we have big hearts."

Taylor shot Daniel a glance. Looking chagrinned, he cleared his throat. "Um…Linda, this is Taylor Milton, a friend of General Miller's. She's here to see the TAL end of things during the shuttle launch."

"Oh, I see. I'm sorry. Forgive my assumption. You two looked like such a couple I simply assumed…I mean I keep telling Daniel he isn't getting any younger and if he ever hoped to make colonel he really needed to get married and I just thought…" Linda trailed off. "I think I should probably just shut up now."

"Good idea." Daniel said. "How's Eddie?"

"Great, great. You guys will have to come to dinner while you're here.

"Linda married an Andalusian," Daniel explained.

"Eduardo's a pediatrician in Seville. People used to call us the Three Musketeers when I was based here."

There it was again, that sense of camaraderie and belonging to a cooperative group that she'd never had.

Linda turned her attention to Taylor. "How is it that you want to be here at a TAL sight? Wouldn't you rather be at Kennedy watching the launch itself?"

"That was my initial thought," Taylor said, "But Daniel convinced that me anyone can watch a shuttle launch at the Cape, but very few people get to see this side of things."

"I see I've stuck my foot in it again." Linda made a zipping motion over her mouth.

"What do you mean?" Taylor asked.

"We'll be performing a precautionary disaster drill. No shuttle has ever made a TAL landing. All the action is at NASA."

"But we treat this as if there *is* going to be an aborted landing," Daniel interjected. "We take it totally serious. We're fully prepared."

"You brought me out here to get me out of the way on launch day, didn't you?" Taylor accused.

A guilty expression crossed his face. The man was incapable of lying.

"Yeah."

"And you were assigned to babysit me."

"Pretty much," he admitted.

Taylor wasn't angry, but she wanted to see him squirm. She'd suspected all along that was the case. She recognized that Daniel and Colonel Grayson resented General Miller intervening on her behalf. But it hadn't mattered to her. And Daniel was right. She could watch the shuttle launch on IMAX and get a close approximation of the live event. What she couldn't duplicate was a week in Spain with Daniel. She was happy to be here.

"Let me show you the control room where we'll be in constant contact with Kennedy during the launch," Linda said and indicated for them to follow her.

"Who's Sandy?" Taylor murmured as she and Daniel walked side by side down the hallway behind Linda.

"My ex-girlfriend."

"The break-up must be pretty recent if your Musketeer friend didn't know about it."

"Fairly recent." He walked with his perfect military stance, not turning his head, not looking at her.

"As in…?"

"We broke up a few weeks before you came to Patrick."

"Ah." She nodded, trying to be cool about this bit of news as well, but she wasn't. She felt miffed and envious and hurt that he hadn't bothered to tell her. "You went from her bed to mine in a matter of weeks. Guess that makes me the rebound girl." She didn't want to sound like a jealous girlfriend, but that's exactly what she sounded like.

Daniel stopped in the middle of the hallway and grabbed Taylor's arm. Linda, the wise woman, kept on walking.

"You know where the control room is, Daniel, join me when you're ready," Linda called over her shoulder.

"Sorry, Taylor," Daniel said. "But you're the one who came onto my turf. You're the one who made it clear you wanted a no-strings-attached affair." His voice sounded as brittle as hard toffee. "I have to hand it to you. At least this time you told me right up front. Not like before when you dropped the bomb on me just as I was about to…"

"About to what?"

"Never mind." He clamped his jaw shut.

He started walking again, but Taylor stayed rooted to the spot. When he realized she wasn't going to follow, he stopped, turned back. "What? We have places to be. Let's go."

She crossed her hands over her chest. "I'm not moving until you finish that sentence."

He marched back toward her, eyes shooting angry sparks. He didn't stop until his boots touched the tips of her Jimmy Choos. "You want to know what I was going to say?"

She tilted her head upward, locked onto his stare with a corresponding glare of her own and sank her hands on her hips. "Yes, I do."

"Are you sure you really, really want to know what I was going to say?"

She didn't blink. "I do."

He laughed but it was not a humorous sound. "Ironic choice of words."

"What are you talking about?"

"The night you screwed my brains out on top of the ROTC building? The night you dumped me?"

"Yes," she said firmly, determined not to slow any weakness. "What about it?"

"I had an engagement ring in my pocket. I was going to ask you to marry me."

His words hit her with the force of a fist knocking squarely into her chin. Her knees wobbled, her stomach jumped. She thought she might be sick right there in the utilitarian, but supremely clean hallway. "Wh-what?"

"Yeah."

"Oh, Daniel."

He'd had a ring. He'd been prepared to ask her to marry him. He'd been bucking tradition, going against his family's wishes, swimming upstream all because she was the woman he'd wanted and she'd ruined it all by breaking up with him, lying to him about how she felt.

Sorrow hit her then. A broken dam of loss and regret.

"You want to know why Sandy left me?"

She shook her head.

"Too bad, I'm telling you anyway. She claims I never got over you, over the way you dumped me. That because of you I wouldn't commit, wouldn't ask her to marry me. That's seriously FUBAR if it's true, and the hell of it is, she might be right."

FUBAR, Taylor thought, the military's way of saying something was messed up beyond all recognition.

Tell him, nudged the voice in the back of her head. *Tell him why you broke up with him. Why you lied.*

But how could she? She'd promised herself she'd never tell.

"Daniel," she whispered and reached out to touch his arm, overcome by a myriad of emotions she didn't want to feel—remorse, sadness, foolishness, anger at both him and herself and worst of all, hope. Dreadful, damaging hope.

He drew back, but there was no mistaking the masculine yearning in his eyes. He'd been hurt badly.

By her.

DANIEL PIVOTED on his heels and headed for the control room, struggling to get his emotions under control.

Doctors do not act like this. Lieutenant Colonels do not conduct themselves in such a manner. He could hear his father's voice in his head, echoed and confirmed by his grandfather's.

He hauled in a deep breath and called on every ounce of reserve he had in him. He had a job to do and he wasn't about to let his personal life interfere. While he might not be able to stop the feelings swirling inside him, he didn't have to let them show. The shuttle launch was scheduled for noon. He and his crew would be ready.

Just before he reached the door leading into the control room, he stopped, turned, held out his hand and in the calmest voice he could muster said, "Come on," to Taylor who was still standing at the far end of the corridor looking lost and forlorn.

She scurried after him.

He left her with Linda while he went outside to greet the medical personnel. He gave his speech. It all went well, and then, as he walked past the extra ground crew gathered from other air bases around the country, he thought he saw someone he recognized. It looked to be the man who'd been taking Taylor's picture the previous evening, dressed as an airman.

He walked closer, but just as he got near enough to identify him, the airman jumped in a jeep with a few other men and they drove off.

You're probably imagining things. How could that tourist get access to Moron?

Still, it bore looking into. As soon as the disaster drill was over, Daniel intended to find out just who in the hell that guy was.

"DEPENDING on how far post-launch the shuttle is, there are various abort routes that can be taken," Colonel Linda Bennett said as she showed Taylor around the control room with full satellite link-up to Kennedy Space Station. Several big-screen television sets showed the Space Shuttle Atlantis resting on the launch pad.

Taylor tried her best to focus on what Linda was saying and keep her mind off Daniel, but he was standing right behind her now and she could smell the starch of his crisply ironed uniform shirt. She kept thinking about the way he'd looked at her in the hallway and about the glorious night they'd just spent together. And she couldn't help but wonder if there was some way they could heal the past and build on the future. Last night didn't have to be about closure. Not if they both decided to change the rules.

Focus on your work. You're here for research. You can have a heart-to-heart with Daniel later.

She had her pocket tape recorder on and she was busying taking notes. Linda had asked her not to shoot any video inside the control room for security reasons and she respected her request.

"If a shuttle needs to be recalled in the first two minutes and twenty seconds after launch, a return-to-landing-site or RTLS is ordered. The TAL mode is an option when the last opportunity for an RTLS had passed, but before the shuttle enters orbit. Based on the trajectory of the shuttle, a TAL site is selected and the shuttle continues across the Atlantic," Linda explained.

The military had so many acronyms it boggled the mind. Taylor jotted them down. Maybe she'd come up with sexy acronyms for her resort.

"For example," Linda continued, "if we were to hear two minutes and twenty seconds after post launch, 'Mission Control states Atlantis, Houston, two-engine Moron,' that could mean an engine had failed and the mission would be aborted. At that point the shuttle would have enough speed to make a Trans-Atlantic landing and the shuttle could fly on its remaining engines into Moron." Linda then went on to brief Taylor about other possible abort scenarios.

After the control-room tour, Linda stayed behind to oversee preparations while Daniel escorted Taylor outside for a close-up view of the runway. There, members of the ground crew were preparing for the drill that would occur simultaneously with the shuttle launch.

"Even before the shuttle launches, ground-support crews at all the TAL sites are standing alert. If a launch abort is called the shuttle could land within just ten minutes from launch to abort landing. The ground crew is highly trained on how to handle an abort, from chemicals present on the shuttle to egress procedures."

"You, too?" Taylor sneaked a glance at him, but his face remained professional, aloof and impassive. No one would have guessed watching them that they'd just spent a sleepless night having wild sex.

"I'm one of the instructors."

She knew he was accomplished. A flight surgeon

and a lieutenant colonel, but it wasn't until she saw all the airmen scurrying around under his command that she fully understood exactly how powerful he was. She had to admit, it was a total turn-on.

The closer it got to liftoff, the more the activities increased. Then, thirty minutes before launch, everyone was in place, standing on alert. Nervous tension snapped in the air; even though the drill was just a formality, the crew acted as if the emergency was a certainty.

"NASA specializes in communication," Daniel said. "They stay in constant contact with the shuttle so responders know what to expect and react accordingly."

The clock was ticking down, all systems were ready. Daniel had a live feed from Kennedy on the satellite phone he carried as did other commanders and crew members. The Atlantis crew of seven was strapped aboard, on their way to the International Space Station. The weather, both at Cape Canaveral and all the TAL sites was perfect. It looked like a go.

The excitement was palpable. Taylor felt that same rush of patriotism she'd experienced flying with the Thunderbirds. But this was different. This time she was with Daniel and they were sharing the rush of being part of something bigger than themselves.

He must have felt the adrenaline rush as well because at one minute to liftoff, he gave her hand a quick squeeze.

They were inside one minute now into the countdown. Taylor swallowed, trying to remember everything Linda and Daniel had told her. NASA would be pressurizing the hydrogen tanks. The deluge water system would be going, reducing the noise of the shuttle as it launched. Reducing the noise was essential to help keep the decibels down to prevent the tiles on the space shuttle from breaking off. The tiles were needed to protect the craft as it came through reentry.

Inside forty-seven seconds. The space shuttle's internal power was activated, indicating they were in the final stages.

Thirty seconds and Daniel squeezed her hand again. She looked at him and a smile passed between them.

"T-minus ten, nine, eight, seven, six…" crackled over the communication system. Taylor held her breath. She didn't think she'd ever felt so much concentrated anticipation and excitement. Well, except for last night in Daniel's arms.

"Five, four, three, two, one and liftoff of Space Shuttle Atlantis."

A cheer went up from the gathered crew, but their job was just beginning as they waited for the magic number that would send them into disaster drill mode.

"Forty seconds into the launch," came the audio from the satellite feed. "Atlantis is approaching speed of one thousand miles per hour."

Throttle up, Daniel had explained, was the point at which the shuttle engines were pushed to maximum power as the craft shoved through the thickest part of the atmosphere.

Firefighters and medical technicians stood at the ready. It was Daniel's job to evaluate their timely response and access the medical conditions of the mock shuttle crew.

Daniel paced back and forth, hands clasped behind his back, every ounce of his concentration focused on the task at hand, looking for all the world like the commanding leader he was. Excitement sent the blood bounding through the pulse at the hollow of her throat. He could have been hers and she'd let him slip through her fingers. And yet...

Her gaze fixed on his profile, the firm jaw, the proud nose, the rugged cheekbones underneath tanned skin. An image rose in her mind of him in a medical field hospital, the determined jaw held rigid as he used his skills to save lives. He'd become a doctor and a decorated Air Force officer because she'd let him go. It had been the right thing.

But inside her heart, it felt so wrong.

"Two minutes and five seconds. The beginning of the solid rocket-booster separation."

The muscles in her body tensed. Taylor had no idea how the person doing the broadcasting was staying so calm. She felt as jittery as if she'd downed a dozen triple espressos.

Then suddenly twenty seconds later, came an announcement that snapped heads around.

"Mission Control states, Houston, two engine, Moron."

No one hestitated. They all sprang into action following the orders Daniel barked out. Instantly the landing strip was massed with people in motion.

Sudden fear quickened her pulse. "Daniel, how—?"

"Out of the way, Taylor. This is no longer a drill. The shuttle's coming down. Here. Now," he spat out and raced around her.

Taylor stood open-mouthed, limbs paralyzed as she watched the team perform in flawless, roboticlike precision. A chill of gooseflesh passed over her.

And then there it was, coming out of the sky, the

space shuttle dropping down, huge and white, like a gigantic wounded swan gliding in for a landing.

She blinked back tears of emotion, unable to believe what she was seeing. Perspiration broke out over her body and she could feel the surge of adrenaline weaken her limbs. Her mouth dropped open, her eyes widened, taking it all in. Stunning.

It sped along the airstrip, carried by nothing more than momentum. She imaged the astronauts inside. What were they thinking? Feeling? Were they as calm as the Air Force crew?

After Daniel had told her to get out of the way, she'd backed up against the building and stood in the shadow of the overhanging eave watching the drama unfold before her eyes. The corrugated metal was cool against her spine, the heels of her shoes digging into the soft asphalt. The air smelled faintly of burning rubber and the sound of controlled, but urgent voices tightened the lump in her throat. Taylor's emotions—anxiety, curiosity, awe and something else she couldn't name— produced a strange taste in her mouth.

An instant after it touched down the shuttle was surrounded by the ground crew, Daniel in the thick of it. He was taller than most of the personnel, and she could find him easily in the crowd.

Through Air Force radio, Taylor picked up that they were monitoring the shuttle for chemical leakage before going in to know how best to address the situation and how it was affecting the astronauts inside.

All she could do was watch, awestruck as the scene unfolded. At some point the medical crew, helmed by Daniel, went into the shuttle.

She held her breath, impaled by jittery apprehension. What if Daniel encountered toxic chemicals while he was inside? Finally, she was forced to take a deep breath and the smell of dust soil, mingled with jet fuel filled her nostrils.

Then Daniel emerged, assisting one of the astronauts down the stairs that had been hurriedly erected. Relief spread through her. Daniel was all right and the space shuttle crew seemed to be operating under their own steam. One by one the seven astronauts were loaded onto the Air Force bus and shuttled to the emergency medical facilities.

Feeling confused and totally out of her element, Taylor stayed out of the way as best she could. She didn't belong here. Finally, she understood Colonel Grayson's resentment at having her underfoot. She was a distraction at best, a liability at most. Daniel was operating on thirty-six hours without sleep on the most challenging event of his life and it was her fault. She'd kept him up all night.

An airman saw her in the spot where she'd taken root. "You're with Doctor Corben, right?"

"Yes."

"He asked me to take you to a quiet place, get you something to eat. He's going to be a while. He's in charge of the astronauts' care until the big brass can fly in from the States."

Taylor nodded.

"He's got a lot of responsibility, your guy."

It was on the tip of her tongue to tell him that Daniel wasn't "her guy," but she said nothing.

"I really admire him," the airman went on as he led

her to an empty cafeteria. "He's a strong leader and an even better doctor."

She was tempted to ask for more details, hungry to hear stories about Daniel.

"Have a seat, miss, and make yourself comfortable. I'll bring you something to eat. It won't be much with the cafeteria closed, just vending machine fare."

"That will suit me just fine." She smiled.

He brought her food and drink. She thanked him before he left, then ate a tasteless, damp egg-salad sandwich and cheese doodles and drank a root beer. Afterward, she sat and prayed—for the shuttle crew, for the service men and women helping them, for Daniel as he performed his duties.

And then she had too much time alone to think.

Useless. She was totally useless. She was frivolous and superficial. She took another sip of root beer, remembering the day before Daniel's graduation. The same day that his mother had come to see her at the house in Austin her father had bought her to use while she attended the University of Texas.

Her private manicurist had been giving her a pedicure when the maid had shown Pamela Corben into the solarium where Taylor lay back in a plush spa chair, her hair doused in rejuvenating essential oils and wrapped in a hot towel. She'd been wearing nothing but a terry-cloth robe, had facial mud on her face and cucumbers over her eyes while the manicurist busily pumiced her heels.

"Mrs. Corben is here to see you," the maid—whose name Taylor didn't even remember—had said.

Taylor plucked off the cucumbers, sat up and peered at the woman whom she'd only met twice. Neither time had she been particularly friendly in spite of Taylor's efforts to win her over.

"Hello, ma'am, it's good to see you." She smiled. "Have a seat. Would you like a pedicure?"

Pamela Corben had looked disapprovingly at Taylor's bare feet. "No, I won't be staying that long."

The tone in her voice had Taylor waving away the manicurist, taking her feet out of the water and reaching for a towel. "Could you give us a minute?"

The manicurist and the maid bowed out of the room.

Taylor got up, slipped her feet into pink spa slippers and tightened the belt of her robe. She waited for Pamela to speak first.

"I'm just going to come out and say what I came here to say."

"All right," Taylor had murmured coolly, but inside, her heart was thumping rapidly.

"I think you're nothing but a silly, spoiled, rich party girl."

A smart retort had risen to her lips, but she'd managed to bite it off. This was Daniel's mother after all.

Pamela Corben came straight to the point. "I know my son cares about you, but you're all wrong for him."

Taylor had taken a deep breath and kept the smile plastered onto her face. "Shouldn't your son be the judge of that?"

Pamela snorted. "You've besotted him with your sexuality. He's young and full of testosterone. He doesn't understand the importance of the right wife when it comes to being a career military physician."

"Excuse me, Mrs. Corben, I mean no disrespect, but since I was a toddler, I've socialized with diplomats, politicians, celebrities, even a king. I think I can handle social protocol."

"You've done it all through the lens of money and privilege. You have no knowledge of rank and military etiquette."

"You could teach me," she'd said, still desperately trying to win the woman over.

"Or we both could save ourselves the trouble."

Taylor had done her best not to show that her hands were trembling. "What are you saying?"

"I want you to break up with my son."

"Why would I do that? I love Daniel."

"Do you?" Her eyes were sharp. "Do you really?"

"Yes, I do," she'd retorted, more hotly than she intended.

"Then prove it by doing what's in his best interest."

"And you think that breaking up with Daniel is in his best interest?"

"Absolutely." She'd clutched her proper matronly leather handbag to her chest like a shield of armor. "Daniel is third-generation Air Force and he wants to be a third-generation doctor. Do you understand the tradition involved? You're simply not military-wife material. You're spoiled and pampered and too loose with your emotions."

Taylor swallowed hard. "Is that all?"

"You're too passionate and opinionated."

"So you believe Daniel would be better off with some milquetoast who picks his socks up off the bathroom floor and happily does his bidding?"

Pamela had drawn herself up tall. "I'm no milquetoast and I'm a military wife."

No indeed. She was a fierce mother bear protecting her cub, even if he didn't need her protection.

"You have no idea the commitment and devotion it takes to be the wife of an Air Force doctor. It takes guts and fortitude. You have to sacrifice your own wants and needs. You must forever and always put his career first. Honestly, are you fully prepared to do that?"

Taylor said nothing. She hadn't looked that far into the future.

"That's what I thought. Here's the thing, Taylor. You're not a bad person. I know my son cares for you a lot and he's a good judge of character, but if you marry Daniel, you'll end up destroying his career. If you truly love him as you say you do, then you'll walk away. You'll let him go to his destiny and you'll be free to pursue yours."

As hard as it was to admit it, Pamela Corben *had* been right. And Taylor had done the right thing in following her advice. Daniel had become a strong and substantial man. A leader. A healer. A man others looked up to. While she…well, she was running sexual-fantasy resorts. She *was* frivolous and insubstantial. Her priorities were centered on fun and making money. Daniel's were centered on saving lives and making the world a better place.

The secret hope that had been budding inside her since that very first day she'd seen him at Patrick Air Force Base—the budding hope that maybe their time together wasn't closure, but rather a new beginning—was completely quashed. Sex was all they'd ever really had. Hot, passionate, stupendous sex, to be sure, but when it got right down to it, they had nothing in common.

Daniel valued honor and tradition and family ties. Taylor valued a good time, great sex and self-reliance. He was part of a team. She was a Brick.

It hit her all at once what she'd been doing. Why she'd come up with the aerospace fantasy in the first place. She'd been trying to recapture the love of her youth. But there was no going back.

She could make love with Daniel until their time together came to an end, but she could never be what he really needed. Not even if she tried for a million years.

Tears, as salty and bitter as the day she'd first broken up with him, formed in her throat, but she swallowed them back. She would not cry. She would accept what she could have. One or two more days with him and then she'd go back to her world and leave him to his.

It was two o'clock in the morning, almost fourteen hours since the shuttle had made its emergency landing. She sat in the dark, fully stewing in her misery, doing nothing to try and chase it away as she once might have. In an odd way the pain nourished her, gave her the strength she needed to do what had to be done.

"Taylor?"

Jerking from her reverie, Taylor blinked up to see Daniel standing beside her. His face was drawn and weary, his eyes bloodshot, beard stubble ringed his jaw. He looked like a conquering hero. He'd been saving lives, affecting the world. She'd been sitting alone in an empty cafeteria feeling sorry for herself.

"The astronauts?" she asked, splaying a palm across her heart.

A slight smile tugged at his lips. "They'll all live to fly again. A few minor injuries, broken bones, a collapsed lung, but everyone is going to be okay."

12

DANIEL was so damned glad to see Taylor, so happy to be able to deliver the news that the astronauts were alive and well. They'd been a part of history today and it was heady stuff.

His eyes were gritty and he was exhausted bone-deep, but one look into her brown eyes and he was reborn. Desire so strong he thought he might die from the power of it wrapped around him.

There was no rational thought involved in what happened next. The base was silent at this hour of the morning. His libido was unchained. "Taylor," he whispered, "you're so beautiful."

She ran a hand through her hair. "I'm sure I look a mess. I haven't brushed my hair or washed my face since—"

"You look like heaven to me."

Her eyes widened and so did her smile, sending his heart careening into his chest. Without another word, he crossed the distance between them and swept her into his arms. "I couldn't have made it through today without you."

"What do you mean? I did nothing to help."

"Yes, you did. Just knowing you were out here,

waiting for me, pulling for me, steadied my hand and gave me strength. Whenever things got rough, I'd just think, *Taylor* and I'd relax."

"You did?" she sounded amazed.

"Absolutely." It amazed him as much as it amazed her. Amazed him and impassioned him. "Like it or not, Taylor, we're connected. There's a bond that even thirteen years apart didn't break. We belong together."

"Belong?" she echoed and her eyes lit up.

"We're a team, you and I." He saw the pulse in her throat quicken, felt her melt against him, heard her exhale, tasted her lips as he lowered his mouth over hers.

"Daniel," Taylor moaned softly and the way she breathed in his name on a sigh pushed him completely over the edge of reason. "Make love to me. Right here, right now. I want you. I need you."

His heart pounded. His hand slipped down to cup her tight, round bottom. His penis strained against his zipper, flourishing from sandstone to solid granite.

Flexing, he curled his fingers into the soft, willing flesh of her buttocks.

You're out of line, whispered his conscience.

But he couldn't stop kissing her or touching her. Her mouth was hot and moist. Her bottom, beneath his palm, was warm and growing hotter with each passing second.

The air vibrated between them.

He was in trouble here, but he did not care.

The erotic promise buried in her kiss made him shudder. The push of her petal-soft lips, the urgency of her breath disoriented him. The curve of her mouth, the swell of her lower lip, the pressure of her teeth.

Did she have any idea how sexy she was?

From the way she thrust her breasts against him, yeah, she had a damned good idea what she was doing, and she was loving every minute of it.

The taste of her was nectar against his tongue. Daniel felt like a primitive creature, responding with nothing more than a savage brain. Everything about Taylor was erotic.

Every whim of Taylor's body triggered his. Every second stirred his imagination. Sensation after sensation washed over him in a rush.

"I need something to hold on to," she said and wrapped both her wrists around his neck. "Can I hold on to you?"

"Baby, I'm here. You can always hold on to me. Don't ever let go," he murmured into the curve of her neck.

Every sensation was amplified, exaggerated—the weight of her body against his legs, the feel of her fingertips stroking his face, the rhythm of her breathing.

In spite of his best intentions not to get emotionally involved with Taylor, he'd failed miserably. How could he not get involved? He hadn't known it, but he'd been involved with her since he was twenty-two years old. She was his first love and he knew in his soul she was his last.

His penis throbbed painfully and he had to squeeze his eyes shut and clench his fists and fight for every shred of control he possessed.

She had gotten to him again. She'd slipped under his radar with her fun-loving attitude and her uninhibited way of being in the world and that saucy grin just begging him to come play.

His senses were on high alert, his body tuned for action. She looked at him with an unusual light in her eyes. It startled him and he appraised her, trying to decipher what was going on inside her head. His body took stock of the world, of this moment.

Relishing the sensation of her mouth against his, Daniel paused, held her close and felt the steady beating of her heart.

Life had taught him to be prudent. His parents had taught him to be honorable and dutiful. Medical school had taught him to be measured and pensive. It was difficult for him to drop his emotional armor and lay down his sword. To allow her inside his fortress. She'd damaged him once and he was still leery.

But she astonished him. Not only by her stunning uniqueness but also by the way she made him feel unique. He confronted what was happening inside him, acknowledging at the same time she might break him all over again.

Though for this moment, this bright and shining moment, their energies were merged. Kissing her, caressing her body with the flats of his palms was a sensory nirvana.

Breathless, she reached for the waistband of his pants.

Daniel kicked off his boots, unbuckled his belt.

He wanted her more than he wanted to breathe, but Daniel suddenly felt bereft and could not really explain why. He appreciated her mastery of sex and longed to play more games with her. But he was afraid she could not move beyond the games.

She undid his fly and stripped off his pants. He flung off his shirt and lay back against the table. She climbed on the table beside him, knelt and traced her fingers over his belly.

Their senses combined, expanded. Taste, sight, smell, sound, touch became a cavalcade of experience. He tasted the saltiness of their pooled flavors. He smelled the sweet richness of her femininity. He heard her raspy, excited breathing. His fingers tingled with the feel of her smooth, satiny skin.

She moaned softly when he cupped her breasts and his erection grew stiffer. During their sex play she produced a condom and helped him put it on.

He liked his body when he was with her. It felt twenty-two again. His muscles seemed stronger, his nerves more alive. He loved her body. What it did. How she responded. He liked the way her back arched when he touched her behind the knees. He loved the way she purred when he skimmed his hands over just the right spots. He thrilled to knead his fingertips along her spine, loved to explore her bones and make her tremble.

Again and again and again he kissed her—thighs, nipples, eyelids, earlobes. He left no patch of skin unkissed. He stroked her soft mound and touched gently her parting flesh.

Daniel felt exposed, shaking with emotion, desperate to be merged with her. He coiled around her, tracing his quivering hands over her body, mapping every part of her like a blind man learning Braille. The little valley between her nose and her lips, the curve of her cheek, the gentle slope of her nose. Luxuriant curves and elegant bones. Taut, lithe muscles. She was a miracle of nature, holding him with her femininity, delighting him with her body.

She pulled his erection into her mouth with long,

lazy, caressing strokes until he was harder than he'd ever been in his life.

"More," she pleaded. "I need more of you."

He sank deeper, joining their bodies as far as they would go. Vibrant impulses shot through him. He felt himself expand. He was under her skin and she was under his, both literally and emotionally.

"Harder," she said. "Faster. Give me everything, Daniel, hold nothing back."

He obeyed because he was helpless to do anything else. He pounded into her, giving her everything she begged for.

Daniel felt as if he were waking up from a long dream. He could see his life for what it was, what it had been, what it could be. He let go of judgment and regret. His body was electrified, while at the same time, he relaxed into the bliss.

Their simultaneous breathing deepened, slowed. They were one breath. One organism. Together they became bigger than the world.

He was aware of everything. The thick darkness sliced only by the light on the vending machine across the cafeteria, the airlessness of the room, the damp heat of their conjoined bodies.

It was in that awareness that he felt the click—the reconnecting of the bond that had once been severed. They were connected in a way he'd never connected with anyone. His habits, goals, agendas and internal scripts fell away. Suddenly, he could see, feel, hear, taste, smell and sense everything in a whole new way.

And in that one miraculous instant, he knew himself to be a changed man, forever altered by loving her.

WE BELONG TOGETHER.

The words Daniel had spoken to her, the words she'd waited a lifetime to hear, were stuck in her brain as they drove back to their hotel in Seville sometime around two in the morning. Daniel had his arm stretched across her shoulders, cradling her as close as the gearshift would allow.

She belonged somewhere.

Her blood sang. Her heart lifted. Her soul soared.

Euphoria.

Then nasty reality slammed her back down to earth. It didn't matter if he thought they belonged together. She knew better. He belonged to the military, to the career he loved and she had no place in that world. He might not realize it now, but he would soon enough if they stayed together.

But she didn't want to think about the future or their past. All she wanted to do was savor this sweet, blissful now. She accepted that this was the most she could ever hope for.

And in that acceptance, she found an odd kind of peace. She felt as if she was floating, drifting on the high of the moment. Tomorrow didn't exist. For this brief span of time, he was hers and they were one.

They arrived at the hotel and hand-in-hand they walked through the lobby to the elevator, the silence between them deep and thoughtful.

Once in their room, Daniel slowly undressed her, planted kisses at her breasts and then dressed her in her nightgown. "Much as I would like to make love to you again, sweetheart, we both need to sleep."

Lines of exhaustion pulled his mouth downward.

His eyes were red-rimmed. His shoulders had lost their military sharpness. Tenderly she touched his cheek, and then lightly ran her fingertips over his mouth. "You were magnificent today."

He shrugged. "Just doing my job."

"You love it, don't you?"

"I do."

"You were born to be an Air Force doctor."

"It does run in the family."

"There's nothing else you'd rather do?"

"Nothing," he assured her.

She knew it, she just needed the confirmation to quell any lingering hope she might be harboring for their future.

He took her hand and led her to bed.

They spooned in the middle of the mattress, their bodies fitting perfectly together. Daniel was behind her, his arm thrown over her waist. Taylor snuggled against him, cocooned in warmth. A bittersweet feeling overtook her. She blinked back sudden tears, closed her eyes and wished desperately that she could freeze this moment to savor for all eternity.

THE FOLLOWING morning Taylor called one of her pilots to fly her home to New York on a small Eros Air jet. Witnessing the history-making TAL landing of the space shuttle—and having sizzling sex with Daniel—had given her all the research she needed for her resort. No point in returning to Cape Canaveral. It was time to take Out of this World Lovemaking out of the planning stages and turn it into reality.

Daniel had to stay at Moron for debriefings. He saw

her off with a kiss and a grin, yet looking at him just about broke her heart. He promised to call and she didn't have the guts to tell him not to.

She told herself she was ready, that she was happy she'd achieved her goal, but inside, she was shattered. She'd thought one last daring sexual romp with Daniel would chase her blues away and bring her some closure.

It had not.

On the contrary she felt more dejected than ever. So when her plane touched down in New York and her executive assistant Heather came to meet her on the tarmac, she welcomed the opportunity to jump right into work.

But one look at Heather's concerned face told her all was not well. "What's up, Heather?"

"We've got trouble." Heather reached out to take Taylor's briefcase as they headed for the waiting limo, while someone from the ground crew hustled to carry Taylor's bags off the plane and deposit them in the vehicle.

"More vandalism?" she asked, slipping on her sunglasses.

"Worse."

Taylor bit down on the inside of her cheek to stave off the attack of nerves threatening to swoop down on her. What now on top of everything else? "Tell me."

"You and Daniel Corben are the lead story on *Celebrity Spy.*"

Celebrity Spy was one of those gossipy entertainment programs that reveled in catching celebrities, dignitaries and VIPS in embarrassing situations. Why would they be interested in her and Daniel?

"What do you mean?" she asked, trying not to create wild scenarios in her head. It was a drawback to having a fertile imagination.

"I've got the segment cued up on the laptop in the limo. I thought you should see it for yourself." Heather held out her hand.

The driver nodded and opened the limo door. "Welcome home, Miss Milton."

"Thank you, Frederick." With her pulse suddenly racing, she forced a smile and slid all the way across the seat so Heather could climb in beside her.

While Frederick drove, Heather started the recorded television feed on the computer she placed on her lap. Taylor took off her sunglasses, and angled the screen for a better view.

"And now for everyone's favorite segment." The cheeky, flamboyantly dressed male announcer winked. "This is Lindel Jones reporting for Exposé Exposed, where we catch the rich and famous in compromising positions and tattletale."

Taylor drew in a shaky breath and put a hand over her mouth.

"What oh-so-chic billionaire airline heiress was caught in flagrante with a top-level Air Force flight surgeon in Moron, Spain, during the momentous aborted space shuttle landing?"

Lindel paused in his monologue, turned and mugged a comic facial expression into a second camera as the shot zoomed in for an intimate effect. He made a finger motion that said; naughty, naughty.

"Yes, Taylor Milton, I'm talking about you. Sweetie, next time you shag someone from team NASA on the cafeteria table, remember everyone has cell phone cameras these days and *Celebrity Spy* has eyes everywhere. From what I can tell it looks like flight surgeon Lieutenant Colonel Dr. Daniel Corben has all the right stuff. Who can blame you, baby." Lindel gave a sexy growl. "Houston, we have liftoff."

Lindel Jones spun back to the wider angle camera. "Is it all just fun and games for Ms. Milton? Or are the rumors that she's doing extensive…um…*undercover*…research for another one of her red-hot fantasy resorts true?"

Oh God, please don't let me throw up.

"Turn it off," she whispered and sank back against the plush leather seat.

"Is it true?" Heather asked, dragging the portable computer from Taylor's lap and shutting it down. "Did you have sex on the cafeteria table with the flight surgeon?"

Taylor nodded imperceptibly.

Heather blew out her breath through puffed cheeks. "I've already called Justin," she said, referring to Taylor's lawyer. "He's meeting us at the office and I've called in a spin doctor, Sebastian Black. He's supposed to be the best in the business."

"We don't need all that."

"Of course we do. You have to fight back."

"If we fight back it will just keep this thing stirred up."

"So? It'll be great PR for the resort."

"So, I want it to die a quiet death. Someone else will have the spotlight tomorrow and they'll forget all about me."

Heather blinked at her. "What happened to you in Spain?"

"What do you mean?" Taylor straightened her skirt, pulling the hem down to her knees.

"You're different." Her assistant canted her head. "I've never known you not to put up a good fight."

Taylor thought of the time she didn't fight for Daniel. "There's been a precedent."

"Excuse me?"

She waved a hand. "Never mind."

Heather's mouth dropped open. "Omigosh."

Taylor sighed. "Omigosh what?"

"I never thought I'd see the day."

"What?"

"I don't believe it."

"Believe what? Spit it out, Heather, What's on your mind?" Taylor asked, trying to keep the irritation from her voice.

"You're in love. You fell in love with that lieutenant colonel."

"Is it that obvious?"

"Uh-huh."

She had fallen in love thirteen years ago and she'd never once stopped loving him. "Now you understand why I want to just let this whole thing blow over? I don't want him getting into any more trouble over me than he already has."

"Where is he?"

"Spain."

"Well, what's going to happen between you two?"

"Nothing," Taylor blurted. "Absolutely nothing. He has his life, I have mine and that's the way it's got to be."

Two days later, on Daniel's return to Patrick Air Force base from Spain, he was ordered into Colonel Grayson's office.

"You wanted to see me, sir?"

"Have a seat," Grayson barked.

Daniel sat.

His superior officer's lips were pressed tightly together and he did not look pleased. Daniel was puzzled. He'd received a glowing commendation from NASA on his performance as chief medical officer during the TAL. He'd expected an attaboy from Cooper Grayson as well.

"I know you just got off the plane from Spain and that you've been tied up with debriefings, so you're probably not aware of what's been happening over here since you left."

"Problems with the medical staff, sir?"

"No, Corben, problems with your personal life, and your failure to complete your assignment as ordered. Not to mention the fact you've disgraced the United States Air Force."

Daniel frowned. "I don't understand."

"Maybe this will clarify things." Grayson picked a remote control off his desk and turned on the flat-screen television set bolted to the wall. Daniel moved his chair around so he could get a better look as Grayson hit the Play button on the digital recorder.

And he got his first glimpse of the program *Celebrity Spies*. By the time the segment was over, a cold sweat bathed his body.

"Your assignment was to take Taylor Milton to Spain and keep her under wraps. Not have sex with her on the cafeteria table!" Grayson bellowed. "It's a flippin' PR nightmare. Not to mention the higher-ups are breathing down my neck wanting to know what the hell she was doing on a military Air Force base during a crucial shuttle launch with my head doctor. I'm caught in the middle. General Miller is pissed off that it leaked out. People are asking questions about how she got access to the base. They want to know why Miller pulled strings. It's thrown his run for political office into jeopardy."

"He should have thought about that before he leaned on us."

"Don't you dare make this about the general. He's got his own mess to deal with. This is about your failure."

Daniel said nothing. What was there to say? Grayson was right. And, all at once, he knew who the tourist had been on the bridge in Seville. Some airman bought off by *Celebrity Spy*.

He could try to find the guy, get even, but it didn't matter. All that mattered was Taylor. He wondered how she was holding up under the stress. His initial instinct was to whip out his cell phone and call her.

Grayson got up, began pacing the floor behind his desk and rubbed a palm over the top of his crew cut head. "My ass is in a vise over this and consequently so is yours."

"I'm sorry I disappointed you, sir."

"Oh, you didn't just disappoint me, Corben." Grayson glowered. "You disappointed yourself. My endorsement that you needed for that promotion? Well, you can kiss it good-bye."

13

DANIEL TRIED calling Taylor but he couldn't get past her gatekeeping executive assistant on her business line and her private cell phone number kept going to voice mail. Clearly, she wanted nothing more to do with him, and he couldn't blame her. Because of him, word had gotten out about her hush-hush research project. It seemed as if he was making a habit of spilling her secrets.

The rest of the day went downhill from there. Colleagues snickered and shot him nudge-nudge, wink-wink glances when they passed him in the hallway. Tag dropped by to razz him with, "Right stuff." And when he got home, he was surprised to find his mother's car parked in his driveway.

He went inside and found her bustling around his kitchen, an apron tied around her waist, delicious smells wafting in the air.

"Hey, Mom," he said, walking over to kiss her cheek. "What are you doing here?"

"Making you a meatloaf."

"What for?" He knew she had to have seen *Celebrity Spies* or, at the very least, someone had told her about it. The timing of her unexpected visit was too coincidental, but he wasn't about to be the one to bring up the subject.

"It's your favorite meal."

"And…?"

"I sprinkled Parmesan cheese on top just the way you like it," she said brightly.

Too brightly.

His mother got excessively chirpy whenever something was bothering her. Her coping strategy, he supposed. "Ma, where's Dad?"

"Visiting your grandfather."

"How come you didn't go with him?"

"I wanted to be here to give you a hero's welcome home from Spain. I'm so proud of you for what you did for those shuttle astronauts."

"I was only doing my job."

"And a fine job you did. Your father heard all about it from his retired NASA buddies down at the club."

She was being so cool that for one minute, Daniel thought maybe she hadn't heard about the other incident that had happened in Spain. But then she dropped her gaze and busily stirred honey into the carrots sautéing in the skillet and he knew that she knew. How come when a guy got around his mother it was like he was suddenly fifteen years old again?

A long moment passed.

"I heard about it, you know." She shoved those carrots around as though they'd insulted her.

He could play dumb, but his mother might spell it out and he didn't want that. "I imagined that you had."

Silence stretched between them. They didn't make eye contact. Daniel walked to the refrigerator and pulled out a beer. If ever a situation called for a dose of liquid courage, this was it.

"I'm sorry it ended up on television. I'm sure it's not easy for either one of you."

"Nope." He twisted the top off, leaned his back against the kitchen counter and took a long swallow. Tucking his left hand underneath his right arm in a protective gesture, he waited.

"I cooked fresh snapped green beans from the market."

"That sounds nice."

Another pause. Another swig of his beer.

"Did Colonel Grayson come down hard on you?"

"Ton of bricks," he replied, and the minute the words were out of his mouth, a picture of Taylor was in his head and an ugly pain was knocking at his heart.

"I didn't know you were seeing Taylor again."

"I wasn't."

"But how…?"

"It's complicated." He picked at the label on his beer bottle.

"You still love her, don't you?"

"Yep."

The wooden spoon in her hand made scraping noises against the bottom of the skillet.

"Ma, you keep that up and we'll be eating strained carrots."

"Right." She dropped the spoon, dropped her hands and finally turned to face him.

He expected to see disapproval on her face, or at the very least, disappointment. But when his mother's eyes met his, that's not what Daniel saw.

She looked contrite. Remorseful. It took him aback.

His mother released a deep breath. "I've got something to confess."

He narrowed his eyes as an uncomfortable feeling knotted up against his chest. "What is it?"

"I made a mistake."

"About what?"

"I was just trying to protect you."

Daniel frowned. "Ma, what did you do?"

Her face blanched. "Taylor didn't tell you?"

Slowly, he shook his head. "Ma?"

"Maybe we'd better sit down."

"Yeah."

They sat at the kitchen table. Daniel wrapped his fist around the sweaty beer bottle. His mother worried the hem of her apron with nervous fingers. Finally, she spoke. "I went to see Taylor on the day before your college graduation."

"Okay," he said warily.

"I shouldn't have done it. It was wrong." She lifted her chin. "But I did it."

He could hardly breathe. "What did you say to her?"

"I…I…asked her to break up with you."

He stared at his mother, her words not fully registering. "What?" he whispered.

A guilty expression drew her lips back as she repeated herself. "I asked her to break up with you. I told her that if she really loved you, then she would prove it by letting you go."

Shock kicked him in the gut. "*Why?* Why would you do something like that to your own son?"

"I knew you were serious about her. That she wasn't some passing fling like I'd hoped," she murmured. "I knew you were going to ask her to marry you. I even found the engagement ring in your things when your father and I were helping you pack to move to Bethesda."

"I thought I'd lost that ring."

"No," she said. "I still have it." Then from the folds of her apron pocket, she produced a small black velvet box. The sight of it tore a hole in the fabric of their relationship.

"You kept it through all these years. Why?"

"Guilt, I suppose."

He picked up the box, cracked it open, started at the modest diamond resting there. He closed it. Fisted his hand around the box, just like he'd fisted it the night Taylor had told him goodbye.

"I'm so sorry."

"Why was my falling in love with Taylor such a threat to you?" he asked, still barely able to wrap his mind around what she was telling him.

"I was afraid she was going to distract you. That you wouldn't follow in your father's and grandfather's footsteps and become an Air Force doctor."

"Would it have been so horrible if I hadn't?"

"It was your destiny."

"Apparently only because you meddled in my life." He pushed back the chair, got to his feet, barely able to restrain his anger.

She got up, too, and tried to reach out to touch his shoulder but he stepped away. "I was wrong. I admit that now. You two were just so young, so mismatched."

He knotted his hands at his side. "But I loved her, Ma. I still love her."

"I figured that." His mother nodded. "When I heard what happened in Spain, I knew there was only one thing that could make my dutiful son behave in such a way and that was true love."

"Let me get this straight. Taylor lied when she said I was nothing more than a fling. And she lied because of you."

"Daniel, I'm *so* sorry." Tears misted his mother's eyes. "Can you forgive me?"

He snorted, raised his palms. "You're my mother and I love you, and I know you thought you were doing the right thing. I will forgive you for this, but right now, I can't even look at you."

Then he turned and walked out the door, leaving behind him the smell of meatloaf and tradition. He walked away from his mother, his mind struggling with what she had done.

He climbed behind the wheel of his jeep, slipped the key into the ignition and then just sat there, poleaxed, the ring box still clutched in his hand. Everything Daniel had ever believed about Taylor fell in on him. His lungs felt frozen and he was having trouble drawing in air.

She didn't break up with him because she hadn't loved him, but precisely because she had.

IN HER New York penthouse apartment, Taylor sat in her luxurious bathtub with the heated spa jets and let the tears flow. After the humiliating piece aired on *Celebrity Spy,* all the networks had picked it up. Serious news reporters questioned why a civilian had been allowed access to sensitive military procedures and inevitably someone had uncovered her connection to General Miller. Uncle Chuck had called her, upset over the turmoil putting his run for political office in jeopardy. She felt badly about that. His dreams were crushed because of her indiscretion. Not good PR for a woman in the business of catering to dreamers.

Human-interest reporters took the ball and ran with it, embellishing the romance of a NASA-connected tryst. Bookings for reservations picked up immediately, packing her resorts' schedules for months to come. It was a fallout she'd neither counted on nor wanted.

She'd had a rotten few days, fending off the curious media hounds, trying to keep her mind off Daniel and on her work. But she couldn't stop thinking about him.

And she couldn't stop the feelings from overwhelming her.

Wretched, jittery, despondent, empty, mournful, guilty. The emotions weighed her down, a sodden blanket of nostalgia, making her wish for what she could never have, for what she could never be.

But as bad as things were for her, she knew they had to be worse for Daniel. She'd put his career on the line with her seductive behavior. She needed to call him, to apologize, express her remorse, but she just didn't have the courage.

Depressed, she pulled up on the drain release with her toes and watched the water swirl down, taking away all her hopes and dreams along with it. She'd picked up the pieces of her life twice—once when she'd broken up with Daniel to please his mother and again when her father had died. She was tough, she could do it a third time.

But the thought made her so weary she could barely move her head. It took ten solid minutes to rouse out of the tub, dry off and slip into a blue silk kimono.

She was brushing her hair when the intercom buzzer rang. She padded to the panel, pressed the button. "Yes, Harold," she said over the speaker to the building's doorman.

"Miss Milton, I hate to bother you at this late hour, but there's a gentleman who insists on seeing you."

"Who is it?"

"A Mr. Daniel Corben."

Daniel was here in New York? Her heart vaulted into her throat. Panic skittered through her. She wasn't ready for this. She hadn't planned on seeing him, especially not tonight. "Tell him it's too late for a visit. Tell him to come to my office tomorrow."

"He's pretty insistent."

"Harold, do you like your job?"

"Yes, ma'am."

"Then do it."

"SHE SAID it's too late to come up," Harold the doorman told him. "Go see her in her office tomorrow morning."

"I don't care what she said. I need to go up there." Daniel moved toward the elevator.

"Sir." Harold stepped to block his path. "Please don't make me call the cops. I hate filling out all that paperwork."

"How long you worked for her, Harold?"

"I worked for Mr. Milton for ten years before Miss Milton inherited the building."

"So you know her pretty well."

"Yes, sir, I do."

"Have you ever seen her in love?"

That made Harold pause. "I don't believe I have."

"You know why?"

Harold shook his beefy head.

"It's because she's been in love with me for thirteen years."

"My, you do think a lot of yourself, don't you?" Harold arched an eyebrow.

"It's true," Daniel insisted.

Harold narrowed his eyes. "Are you the one who got her into trouble with *Celebrity Spy?* She's very upset over it."

"Yeah, and I'm really sorry about that, but you've got to let me go up there."

"Sir, I really can't."

"Harold, have a seat." Daniel pointed at the chair behind the bank of security cameras. "I've got something to tell you that I know will change your mind. And it all starts with this little box."

Daniel set the ring box on the desk and launched into his story….

TWENTY MINUTES later, Daniel was knocking on Taylor's door. He stood to one side so she couldn't see him through the peephole.

"Harold," Taylor called from the other side of the door, "Is that you?"

Daniel coughed loudly.

Taylor opened the door.

Their eyes met.

"Oh, no, you don't," she said and started to shut it again, but he jammed his foot inside.

"Taylor, we have to talk."

"I have nothing to say to you right now."

"I know you're upset over this *Celebrity Spy* nonsense."

"I do not want to talk about it. Harold is so fired."

"Don't take it out on him." Daniel pushed on the door, forcing it open enough for him to get the rest of his body inside. He came toward her.

She backed up. "Dammit, I don't want you here."

"Can't we just talk about this?" He heard the tears in her voice but he didn't understand why she was so upset. Yes, the *Celebrity Spy* thing was terrible, but it wasn't the end of the world.

"No. Just go."

He reached for her, but she twisted away from him. "Taylor, please, just hear me out."

She tossed her head, marched toward the door.

"You're not walking out." Daniel strode after her.

"The hell I'm not."

At the door, he snagged her elbow and hauled her back into the room. He had to do something to get through to her, even if it meant playing hardball. He couldn't lose her again. "You can't walk out. It's your apartment and you're wearing a bathrobe."

"Let go of me." Taylor's eyes snapped fire and she turned to plant both palms against his chest. She pushed hard, but he did not release her.

"Like it or not, we're talking this thing through."

"There's nothing to discuss."

"I let my hurt feelings stop me from getting to the bottom of why you lied to me thirteen years ago. It was the biggest mistake of my life. I'm not making it again."

"I didn't lie."

"Yes, you did, and you're lying about lying. No matter

what you said that night on the roof of the ROTC building, I meant more to you than just some springtime fling."

"You didn't," she denied, twisting in his arms, her eyes growing wide.

"I'm going to prove it to you. To me."

"What are you going to do?" she whispered and lifted her defiant little chin.

"What I should have done the night you lied." He saw the muscles in her throat quiver, recognized she was running scared. But at the same time, her pupils dilated, telling him she was as turned on as she was nervous. She loved him, but she was terrified to admit it, afraid that if she said the words she'd break apart.

That was all he needed to know. Using his body to block her from the door, he maneuvered her against the wall, raised her arms over her head and pinned her wrists into place.

He lowered his head.

She turned away, pretending that she did not want his kiss. But he knew better. He saw her nipples bead hard, heard her throaty, in-drawn breath.

He took her lips more roughly than he intended, but she excited him so damn much he barely knew what he was doing. She thrashed, resistant. He let go of her wrists, but he did not pull his mouth from hers. He kissed her with thirteen years' worth of pent-up emotion.

Daniel knew the moment she gave in. Her jaw loosened and she let his tongue inside her mouth with a soft, surrendering moan in the back of her throat. He ground his pelvis against hers as he kissed her, running his palms along her narrow waist.

One hand strayed upward, while the other held her

steady. His fingers pinched her nipples through the silk of her kimono. She writhed beneath him. Her movements cemented his arousal.

He slipped the robe off her shoulders. She helped him, wrestling it off, tossing it to the ground. Immediately, he pressed his lips to her skin, kissing his way down the column of her throat and lower to her full, lush breasts.

But before he could capture one perky pink nipple between his teeth, she sandwiched his face between her palms and raised his head up to stare him in the eyes.

Her gorgeous golden-red hair tumbled around her shoulders, a mussed riot of humidity-induced curls. "What do you want from me?"

"If I have to spell it out, clearly I'm not getting my interest across to you."

Her breath was ragged. "We can't pick up where we left off in college."

"Of course not," he said. "I've changed. You've changed."

"Not enough," she remarked. "You're still in the military and I'm—"

"Passionately opinionated."

"Yes. My passion, my drive, my inability to follow rules will ruin your career. Ruin us."

"It won't."

"It will." She looked furious and he couldn't figure out why. "You want me?"

"You know I do."

"Fine, great, you can have me." Her trembling hands went for the button on the waistband of his pants, her chest rising and falling rapidly.

"No, no, no, that's not how I want it," he said, although

at this point he wanted her so bad it was all he could do to keep from taking her quickly and roughly. "I want all of you. Not just your body. I want your heart, your mind, your soul."

"Greedy bastard."

"Damn straight." He shoved his fingers through the hair at the nape of her neck, tilted her head back and forced her to look at him. "Now you tell me what *you* want."

Her breath was ragged. "I want you to let me leave."

"Do you?" He peered into her eyes. "Do you really?"

Her bottom lip trembled. "No," she whispered.

He pressed his mouth to her ear, his fingers still tangled in her hair. "Tell me."

She shivered. "I—I…want you to suck my nipples."

"Sex. That's what you want from me?"

She nodded.

"Okay, if that's what it takes to get you to where you need to be, then I'll give you all the sex you want."

He caressed her body eagerly with his hands, his mouth. Taylor was just as frantic, clawing at his shirt, popping off buttons. In a matter of seconds they were both naked and rolling around on the floor like wild things.

"Do me, Daniel. Do me now."

He lay on his back, pulled her astride his waist. He lightly clasped her hips, helping her to kneel above him so that his penis nudged at the entrance of her opening. She placed her hands flat on his chest and slowly lowered herself down, until an inch of him had slipped inside her.

She whimpered. "More."

"You want me?"

Solemnly she nodded.

"Then you've got to tell me what I need to hear, Taylor. Tell me what you should have told me thirteen years ago."

Her lips moved but she couldn't seem to force the words out.

"No?"

"Daniel…" she whispered and tried to sink down deeper on his penis but he held her firmly speared on just the tip of him.

"I know it's hard for you to admit your feelings. I know you've got some kind of weird psychology going on. But you've got to trust me, Taylor. Trust me. You got that?"

She bit her lip to keep from moaning, but didn't succeed. Neither did Daniel. Their moans melted together as one, melodic and harmonious.

"You want more?"

"Uh-huh."

"Say it."

She tossed her head.

"Okay," he said. "You can't tell me, so I'm going to tell you. I love you, Taylor Milton. I've loved you since I was twenty-two years old. I tried to deny it. I picked up the pieces of my life and moved on, but I never forgot. And when I saw you again, I knew it was true. I love you and I'm going to keep loving you until I'm a hundred and twenty-two."

"What happens when you're a hundred and twenty-three, will you stop loving me then?"

"That's what this is about, isn't it? You're afraid that if you love me, you'll lose me?"

She nodded and looked so vulnerable it tore him in two.

He released his hold on her waist then, let her sink down on his shaft.

She pushed down even further.

"That's the way, baby. Go deeper."

She kept going until his cock was almost fully inside her. Swiveling her hips at the last moment, she lifted herself off him. He groaned with frustration. Then she sank down again until he was completely within her.

Daniel reached down and rubbed her sensitive clit with his thumb. Her moan went up an octave and she arched her hips.

"Tell me. Just say it. I swear I won't ever leave you. I swear it…. Just tell me."

"I…" She licked her lips. "I love you, Daniel."

He pulled her face down to him and covered it in kisses. "There you go, that's my girl. I love you, too, Taylor. Love you."

Taylor was overcome by emotions, unable to believe she was finally able to voice the feelings she had held at bay for most of her adult life. "I love you. I love you. I love you."

Once started, she couldn't seem to stop. With every movement she made, she breathed the words like a prayer. "I love you, Daniel Corben. I love you."

He ran his hands through her hair, played with her tits. "That's it. That's it."

Crazed with blind love, she raised and lowered herself on and off him repeatedly, enjoying the drag of her sensitive skin against the hardness of his shaft. She was oblivious to how much time went by as she rode him. Seconds. Minutes. Hours. She was lost in sensation. Lost in love. Aware of nothing else but the supreme rightness of this moment.

"Love you, Daniel. Love you, love you, love you."

His fingers dug deeply into her hips and she heard him begging. "I'm going to come. Move faster, baby. You've got to move faster."

His words spurred her on until her breasts were bouncing furiously. Her release was just out of reach and she wasn't sure what she needed to do to grab it.

Daniel leaned up and nibbled one of her nipples. The shock of it made her whimper and caused her womb to contract.

Then it happened, strong as an earthquake. She was hurtling over a cliff with each squeeze of pleasure that racked her body. Daniel groaned, shuddered and she knew he was falling with her.

They landed together, Daniel's arms clasped around her, her head resting on his chest, listening to the frantic lub-dub of his heart against her ear.

Barely able to catch her breath, she closed her eyes, felt his love seep all the way through her. His penis was still tucked within her. It twitched and swelled, growing again, wanting more from her.

She looked down at him. He looked up at her and they said the words together. The words they should have said to each other all those years ago.

"I love you."

SOMETIME LATER they moved to the bed and lay with the covers piled up over them, stroking their fingers over each other.

"I've got something for you," Daniel said.

"A present? For me?"

"Hang on." He got up and padded into the living room. A minute later he returned holding something behind his back.

Taylor sat up in bed, clutching the sheet to her bosom. "What have you got there?"

He crawled back up on the mattress beside her, held out the ring box. She inhaled deeply. "Daniel…"

"It's the one I was going to give to you that night on top of the ROTC building."

"Oh, Daniel." Tears fill her eyes and her heart ached for all they'd suffered, all the time together that they'd lost. If only she had listened to her own heart instead of her father's gloomy philosophy on love and Daniel's mother's prejudiced advice.

"No regrets," he murmured, a misting of tears in his own eyes. "Fresh start. You and me. We belong together. We've always belonged together. Yes, we had a detour, but we're here now and that's all that counts."

She picked up the ring. "It's inscribed." She turned on the bedside lamp and read the words. "To Brick, you'll always be the one."

"Daniel." This time she did cry, the tears rolling down her cheeks in soft plops.

He leaned over, kissed away the tears. "Don't cry, babe, I know the ring is pretty small but it was all I could afford in college."

"I'm not crying over the size of the ring, you doofus. It's the perfect size, the perfect ring."

It was the perfect size. Not big and ostentatious, but understated and elegant. Even without a jeweler's loupe, she could tell the quality was exquisite. Just like Daniel.

"You *are* giving it to me, right?"

"Thirteen years too late, but, yeah."

"You never took it for a refund?"

He shook his head.

"Why not?"

Shrugging, he said, "I guess deep down inside somewhere I still clung to the hope you'd come back to me. Guess that makes me the world's biggest fool. I stuck it in the back of a drawer. Then I thought I'd lost it. Apparently, my mother found it and guilt had her hanging onto it."

"How is she going to feel about this? About us?"

"She's the one who told me she'd made a mistake."

"What about your promotion?"

He made a face. "That's gone, but you know what? I don't care. All my life I've been doing what everyone else wanted me to do. But I'm done with that. From now on, I'm following my heart."

"And where does that lead?"

"To you."

"Are you sure?"

"I've never been more sure of anything in my life."

Taylor touched the ring, not fully able to believe this was happening. Her greatest fantasies come true.

He took the ring from her, and, naked as the day he was born, got down on one knee. "So what do you say, will you marry me, Taylor Milton?"

She stared deeply into his eyes and knew she'd finally found where she belonged. "Yes, Daniel Corben, I'll marry you."

Then she pulled him up onto the bed with her and made love to him all night long.

Epilogue

NEWLY MINTED Colonel Dr. Daniel Corben looked down the aisle as his bride-to-be came toward him. She was on General Miller's arm and "Wedding March" was playing.

The ceremony was thirteen years in the making, but one look at Taylor's beautiful, smiling face and he knew it was worth the wait. Finally, they were going to get their happily ever after.

The day after Daniel had asked her to marry him, Taylor called *Celebrity Spy* and gave them an exclusive interview to tell them the story of their romance. And then she called *The New York Times* to announce their engagement. She gave her Uncle Chuck all the credit for their reunion.

General Miller came off looking like a matchmaker reuniting two long-lost lovers, and the positive media coverage caused his popularity to skyrocket. He intervened on Daniel's behalf with Colonel Grayson and that, combined with recommendations from Linda Bennett for his performance during the shuttle's aborted landing, earned him his promotion.

In deference to the controversy she'd stirred up, Taylor decided to forgo creating Out of this World

Lovemaking as her fourth resort. Besides, it had been her particular fantasy and she'd achieved it—in spades. Instead, she decided on Make Love Like a Movie Star in tribute to her father, but she was only going to feature movie scenarios with happy endings. No *Casablanca,* no *Gone With the Wind,* no *Tale of Two Cities.* She was scouting a site for the resort in Hollywood as well as moving her head offices to Florida.

Pamela Corben had apologized to Taylor in person and Taylor forgave her unconditionally. Because she had no mother, she turned to Pamela for advice on planning the wedding.

Daniel was pleased to get a call from Sandy, telling him she was excited to hear he'd reunited with Taylor, and she had a bit of good news herself. She'd found her own true love—Anthony Taglioni—and they were getting married. Daniel and Taylor laughed to think of Tag finally having his wings clipped.

TAYLOR'S STEADY GAZE met Daniel's. She'd been so mistaken about what love meant. Her father had done what he thought best, preparing her to lose love. What he hadn't taught her was how to embrace love with all her heart.

But now she had Daniel to teach her that lesson.

She'd been running from life. Hiding behind fantasies, but it had done no good. Having fun, living in the moment, avoiding pain had limited her growth. Now that she had released the need to hide from the pain of life, she had found the belonging, the acceptance she'd been aching for. The resulting calmness had purified her, brought her closure.

Reunion had brought healing, mended their troubled souls. Love didn't cause grief but healed it. She was unafraid of the future.

Together, she and Daniel had all the right stuff.

* * * * *

Celebrate 60 years of pure reading pleasure
with Harlequin®!

Step back in time and enjoy a sneak preview of an
exciting anthology from Harlequin® Historical with
THE DIAMONDS OF WELBOURNE MANOR

This compelling anthology features three stories
about the outrageous Fitzmanning sisters. Meet
Annalise, who is never at a loss for words… But
that can change with an unexpected encounter in
the forest.

Available May 2009
from Harlequin® Historical.

"**I**'m the illegitimate daughter of notoriously scandalous parents, Mr. Milford. Candidates for my hand are unlikely to be lining up at the gates."

"Don't be so quick to discount your charms, my dear. Or the charm of your substantial dowry. Or even your brothers' influence. There are as many reasons to marry as there are marriages."

Annalise snorted. "Oh, yes. Perhaps I shall marry for dynastic reasons, or perhaps for property or influence. After all, a loveless, practical marriage worked out so well for my mother."

"Well, you've routed me on that one. I can think of no suitable rejoinder." Ned rose to his feet and extended his hand. "And since that is the case, let me be the first to wish you a long and happy spinsterhood."

Her mouth gaped open. And then she laughed.

And he froze.

This was the first time, Ned realized. The first time he'd seen her eyes light up and her mouth curl. The first time he'd witnessed her features melded together in glorious accord to produce exquisite beauty.

Unbelievable what a change came over her face. Unheard of what effect her throaty, rasping laughter had on his body. It pounded a beat upon his ear, quickly taken up by his pulse. It echoed through him, finally residing in his stirring nether regions.

So easily she did it, awakened these sensations within him—without any apparent effort at all. And she had called him potentially dangerous? Clearly the intelligent thing for him to do would be to steer clear, to leave her to the tender ministrations of Lord Peter Blackthorne.

"You were right." She smiled up at him as she took his hand and climbed to her feet. "I do feel better."

Ah, well. When had he ever chosen the intelligent path?

He did not relinquish her hand. He used it to pull her in, close enough that he could feel the warmth of her. "At the risk of repeating Lord Peter's mistake and anticipating too much—may I ask if you'll be my partner in battledore tomorrow?"

Her smiled dimmed. Her breath came a little faster. His own had gone shallow, as if he'd just run a race—and lost. He ran his gaze over the appealing lift of her brow and the curious angle of her chin. His index finger twitched.

"I should like that," she said.

His finger trembled again and he lifted it, traced the pink and tender shell of her ear, the unique sweep of her jaw. Her pulse leaped beneath her skin, triggering his own. Slowly he tilted her chin up, waiting for her to object, to step back, to slap his hand away.

She did none of those eminently sensible things. Which left him free to do the entirely impractical thing.

Baby soft, the skin of her lips. Her whole body trembled when he touched her there.

He leaned in. Her eyes closed, even as she stood straight against him, strung as tight as a bow. He pressed his mouth to hers. It was a soft kiss, sweet and chaste. And yet he was hot and hard and as ready as he'd ever been in his life.

She drew back a little. Sighed. Their breath mingled a moment before she slowly backed away.

"Oh," she breathed. Her dark eyes were full of wonder and something that looked like fear. He took a step toward her, but she only shook her head. His outstretched hand fell to his side as she turned to disappear into the wood. This was the first time, Ned realized. The first time, since he'd come to the house party at Welbourne Manor, that he'd seen her eyes light up.

* * * * *

Follow Ned and Annalise's story in May 2009 in
THE DIAMONDS OF WELBOURNE MANOR
Available May 2009 from Harlequin® Historical

Available in the series romance section,
or in the historical romance section, wherever
books are sold.

**We'll be spotlighting a different series
every month throughout 2009
to celebrate our 60th anniversary.**

Look for Harlequin® Historical in May!

Celebrations begin with
a sumptuous Regency house party!

Join three scandalous sisters in

**THE DIAMONDS OF
WELBOURNE MANOR**

Glittering, scintillating, sensual fun
by Diane Gaston, Deb Marlowe
and Amanda McCabe.

**60 years of Harlequin,
600 years of romance
in Harlequin Historical!**

You're invited to join our Tell Harlequin Reader Panel!

By joining our new reader panel you will:

- Receive Harlequin® books—they are FREE and yours to keep with no obligation to purchase anything!
- Participate in fun online surveys
- Exchange opinions and ideas with women just like you
- Have a say in our new book ideas and help us publish the best in women's fiction

In addition, you will have a chance to win great prizes and receive special gifts! See Web site for details. Some conditions apply. Space is limited.

To join, visit us at
www.TellHarlequin.com.

THBPA0108

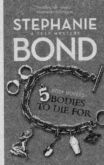
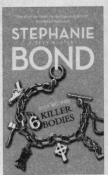

REQUEST YOUR FREE BOOKS!

2 FREE NOVELS PLUS 2 FREE GIFTS!

HARLEQUIN®

Blaze™

Red-hot reads!

YES! Please send me 2 FREE Harlequin® Blaze™ novels and my 2 FREE gifts (gifts are worth about $10). After receiving them, if I don't wish to receive any more books, I can return the shipping statement marked "cancel". If I don't cancel, I will receive 6 brand-new novels every month and be billed just $4.24 per book in the U.S. or $4.71 per book in Canada. Shipping and handling is just 25¢ per book. That's a savings of 15% or more off the cover price! I understand that accepting the 2 free books and gifts places me under no obligation to buy anything. I can always return a shipment and cancel at any time. Even if I never buy another book, the two free books and gifts are mine to keep forever.

151 HDN ERVA 351 HDN ERUX

Name	(PLEASE PRINT)	
Address		Apt. #
City	State/Prov.	Zip/Postal Code

Signature (if under 18, a parent or guardian must sign)

Mail to the **Harlequin Reader Service:**
IN U.S.A.: P.O. Box 1867, Buffalo, NY 14240-1867
IN CANADA: P.O. Box 609, Fort Erie, Ontario L2A 5X3

Not valid to current subscribers of Harlequin Blaze books.

Want to try two free books from another line?
Call 1-800-873-8635 or visit www.morefreebooks.com.

* Terms and prices subject to change without notice. Prices do not include applicable taxes. N.Y. residents add applicable sales tax. Canadian residents will be charged applicable provincial taxes and GST. Offer not valid in Quebec. This offer is limited to one order per household. All orders subject to approval. Credit or debit balances in a customer's account(s) may be offset by any other outstanding balance owed by or to the customer. Please allow 4 to 6 weeks for delivery. Offer available while quantities last.

HB09R

Harlequin® Historical
Historical Romantic Adventure!

If you enjoyed reading
Joanne Rock in the
Harlequin® Blaze™ series,
look for her new book
from Harlequin® Historical!

THE KNIGHT'S RETURN
Joanne Rock

Missing more than his memory,
Hugh de Montagne sets out to find his
true identity. When he lands in a small
Irish kingdom and finds a new liege in the
Irish king, his hands are full with his new
assignment: guarding the king's beautiful,
exiled daughter. Sorcha has had her heart
broken by a knight in the past. Will she be
able to open her heart to love again?

Available April
wherever books are sold.

COMING NEXT MONTH
Available April 28, 2009

#465 HOT-WIRED Jennifer LaBrecque
From 0–60
Drag racer/construction company owner Beau Stillwell has his hands full trying to mess up his sister's upcoming wedding. The guy just isn't good enough for her. But when Beau meets Natalie Bridges, the very determined wedding planner, he realizes he needs to change gears and do something drastic. Like drive sexy, uptight Natalie absolutely wild...

#466 LET IT RIDE Jillian Burns
What better place for grounded flyboy Cole Jackson to blow off some sexual steam than Vegas, baby! Will his campaign to seduce casino beauty Jordan Brenner crash and burn, once she discovers what he really wants to bet?

#467 ONCE A REBEL Debbi Rawlins
Stolen from Time, Bk. 3
Maggie Dawson is stunned when the handsomest male *ever* appears from the future, insisting on her help! Cord Braddock's out of step in the 1870s Wild West, although courting sweet, sexy Maggie comes as naturally to him as the sun rising over the Dakota hills....

#468 GOING DOWN HARD Tawny Weber
When Sierra Donovan starts receiving indecent pictures of herself—with threats attached—she knows she's going to need help. But the last person she needs it from is sexy security expert Reece Carter. Although, if Sierra's back has to be against the wall, she can't think of anyone she'd rather put her there....

#469 AFTERBURN Kira Sinclair
Uniformly Hot!
Air force captain Chase Carden knows life will be different now that he's back from Iraq—he's already been told he'll be leading the Thunderbird Squadron. Little does he guess that his biggest change will come in the person of Rina McAllister, his last one-night stand...who's now claiming to be his wife!

#470 MY SEXY GREEK SUMMER Marie Donovan
A wicked vacation is what Cara Sokol has promised herself, although she has to keep her identity a secret! Hottie Yannis Petridis is exactly what she's looking for *and* he's good with secrets—he's got one of his own!

www.eHarlequin.com

HBCNMBPA0409